Sweet Carolina

Roz Lee

Sweet Carolina
Copyright © 2012 by Roz Lee
All Rights Reserved
ISBN: 1477539190

ISBN13: 978-1477539194

For Sarah,
whose love of the sport
inspired this story.

.

ACKNOWLEDGMENTS

Writers write because they have no choice. The stories simply must be told. It's a compulsion few non-writers can understand. Even though I'm not sure they really comprehend why I do this, I have to thank my family for their unwavering support. Without their steadfast encouragement, faith and patience, I never would have found the courage to unleash my stories on the general public.

This book, in particular, would never have come about without my daughter's enthusiasm for the sport. Her insistence that I should write a story about a racecar driver is the reason this book exists. So, thank you, Sarah for putting the idea in my head.

The wonderful cover is the work of Talina Perkins, a.k.a. Superwoman. Thanks, Talina, for your support, your talent and your friendship.

To the fabulous people who take time out of their busy lives to read my stories, I thank you from the bottom of my heart.

*

Chapter One

"On your right."

"Stay low."

"Clear."

"Hold steady."

Dell listened to the voice in his ear. Earl was one of the best spotters in racing and Dell would have to be crazy not to pay attention. One hundred and eighty miles per hour doesn't leave much room for error. Hell, there wasn't any room for error. The 14 car sped past on his right, leaving Dell looking at his bumper. He loosened his fingers on the steering wheel to keep blood flowing, then curled them back into a tight grip. His car inched up the track. The wall zoomed past, close. Too close.

"I'm tryin', Earl," he answered. "Car's loose. I don't know if I can hold speed and make it through the turn."

"Stay low," Earl admonished.

Dell fought the car through curve two, narrowly missing the wall as the rear of the car lost its grip on the track and pulled him up the embankment.

"Go back low."

"Fuck, I'm tryin'," Dell said. "Who the hell built this car? The backend is all over the place."

"Hang in there, Dell. We'll pit on caution and adjust the track bar."

*

Dell battled the car through two more turns, barely keeping off the wall in turn four. He coaxed a bit of extra power out of the car on the straightaway, caught some air drafting off the car in front of him, and throttled back in turn one again, fighting to keep the backend from dragging him ass-backwards up the embankment and into the wall.

"Shit, Dell. Go low. Clear left. Hug the stripe."

"I would if I could," he said through gritted teeth. "Car needs a rebuild. Piece of fucking shit."

"Engineers are working on the problem, Dell."

"Hi, Ray," Dell greeted his crew chief. "What the hell happened? The car was perfect in qualifying."

"Don't know, but we'll have a fix when you pit."

"If I make it that long. Damn thing's dragging me all over the track."

"Right." Earl again.

Dell glanced in the rearview mirror and saw the car coming up on his right side.

"Got it."

Shit. "Where are we?" Dell asked.

"Fifteenth, and slipping."

Well, fuck. The first race of the season, the Daytona 500, and he was driving a piece of shit that didn't have a preacher's prayer of winning. At this rate, finishing would be a long shot. It was only a matter of time before the car asserted its inclinations and dragged him into the wall, or worse, into another car. The 35 car passed and dropped down the track, forcing Dell to throttle back.

"Clear."

"Yeah, I see." Fuck.

"Ten laps." Earl called the milestone out.

Jesus. Only ten laps? "Roger," he acknowledged. "Where's a fucking caution when you need one?" he asked.

"Patience, Dell," Earl said. Such an idiotic statement didn't warrant a response. Dell wrestled the steering wheel, willing the car to follow.

"You've got a tail," Earl said.

Dell glanced in the mirror. Shit. What the fuck would Warner want to draft off him for? Dell couldn't think of a single reason anyone on the track would draft off a car the driver couldn't control, and it had to be obvious to everyone the car was driving him, not the other way around.

"Fuck."

"Hold," Earl admonished.

"Like I have any fucking control," Dell answered. "What the hell does he think he's doing?" Daytona was one of two tracks where bump drafting, catching a free ride, so to speak, from the driver in front of you, was allowed. It could be a mutually beneficial maneuver, causing both cars to go faster, but the last thing Dell needed was to go faster. With the recent rule changes, it wasn't wise, or necessary to draft for the entire race. Most drivers saved the maneuver for when they or a teammate needed a boost. If it had been anyone other than Richard Warner on his tail, he might have been grateful.

His car lurched when Warner eased up on his bumper, pushing, nudging. Dell reacted, braking, engaging the clutch and using his heel to rev the engine – keeping the RPM up. The car responded, and pushed by the car kissing its bumper, accelerated. Dell's eyes flicked to the control panel and back. He cringed at the increase in speed. Shit. He re-engaged the gears and held on for the ride.

His fingers tightened on the wheel and his arms ached with the effort to keep the car on the track. Seconds. Flying, fleeting, seconds. Warner was going to take him out of the race. It was the only reason Warner could have for drafting at this stage of the game.

Dell ground his teeth as he approached turn one.

"Clear right," Earl said.

Fuck. Warner nudged his bumper. The rear end of Dell's car lost its tenuous hold on the asphalt. He turned into the slide, trying to bring the car back under his control. The sound of crumpling metal penetrated his sound-muffling headphones as the car hit the wall. He spun out of control down the thirty-one degree embankment at one hundred and eighty miles per hour.

Dell fought for control and prayed no one would hit him as he spun in dizzying circles. His car came to a halt at the bottom of the turn, untouched, but mangled from his close encounter with the wall.

"Caution's out," Earl informed him.

"Fuck that." Dell shifted into gear and throttled up. Warner had fucked with him one too many times. It ended here. Now.

If Dell was out of the race, Warner was going out too.

"Damnit, Dell, pit. Now." Ray's usually calm voice was anything but.

"Shit, Dell. Pit," Earl entreated. "Fix the car, then we'll beat Warner."

Dell ignored both men and steered what was left of his car back on the track. He racked up a half-dozen penalties as he sped around the track, passing the cars slowed under the yellow caution flag. Warner wasn't going to get by with it, not this time. This time he would pay.

Turn four. Perfect. In the aftermath of Dell's spin, Warner wormed his way into the front of the pack and now cruised sedately three positions behind the pace car. Dell caught the look of surprise on Warner's face as he traded paint with him. Satisfaction brought a smile to Dell's face right before he wrenched the wheel to the right and drove Warner's car hard into the wall.

Dell eased off the throttle and dropped behind Warner. Warner over-corrected and his car dropped toward the bottom of the track.

"Oh, no you don't," Dell mumbled as he cut low, accelerating in time to ram Warner in the rear left panel, sending him back up the track toward the wall. Dell followed, keeping his right bumper tight against Warner's car, pushing.

Warner hit the wall again and spun. Dell throttled back, but not in time. Warner clipped him and sent him spinning down the embankment in turn four. Metal shrieked against metal. Dell jolted as one car rammed him on the left. Another plowed into him from the right. Smoke filled the interior, blinding him. Not that it mattered. His car was destroyed, steering a luxury no longer available. Dell braced for impact as his car careened out of control, spinning in circles like a giant, lethal top.

Ray's voice in his ear broke the unnatural silence. "You okay?"

Dell considered the question. He was alive. He mentally took stock of his appendages. All present and accounted for. "Yeah. I'm okay," he said. "Getting out now."

He unhooked the six-point seat restraint and reached up to disconnect his helmet from the communications and cooling systems. A moment later, he stood beside his mangled car. He'd come to a stop on the grass, smack-dab in the middle of the giant painted letters that spelled out "Daytona."

Before he took his helmet off, the crash team arrived and hustled him into the back of an ambulance. As they shut the door, he caught a glimpse of his car. Well, fuck. That wasn't going to go over well. Even if it were a piece of shit, it cost a fortune to build. Turning

4

it into scrap metal ten laps into the first, and arguably biggest race of the season wasn't going to win him any points with the team owner.

❧

"You're a menace, C.J. Your daddy must be turning in his grave."

Dell Wayne leaned all six feet of his aching body against the wall, his arms crossed over his broad chest, and fists clenched as the power behind AARA (American Auto Racing Association) stewed over this latest infraction. Why the hell they thought he'd care if his old man spun in his grave, he couldn't fathom. He just wanted to get this over with, and go. The race was over, for him, at least. The Daytona 500 would go down as a DNF – Did Not Finish. All because of Dickhead Warner.

"Dell. My name is Dell," he reminded the old man.

"Caudell Wayne, Junior don't you get smart with me, young man. I've known you since you were in diapers, and I'll damned well call you whatever I want. Your daddy called you C.J., and as far as I'm concerned, that's your name."

Dell held his tongue. What did a man have to do to prove himself? Apparently, there wasn't a damn thing he could do. He'd be Caudell Junior for the rest of his life. He'd never measure up to his old man in the eyes of these people, just like he never measured up in his old man's eyes. What the hell? He shook his head. Why did he even try?

"What do you want from me?"

"We want to know what happened out there today. Are you trying to kill yourself, C.J.? Or are you trying to kill the other drivers?"

He flinched on the inside. His fire suit might as well have been wool. His skin itched, and he couldn't wait to get out of it, the fire suit, or his skin, either one, and out of this place – away from the pity and disapproving looks. "It was an accident," he answered. "That asshole, Warner, clipped my bumper and sent me into the wall."

"And instead of pitting, you went after him. You destroyed his car, and damned near killed him. If this was a few years ago, before the new safer barriers, you would have killed him."

Dell smirked at the irony of it. Nobody blinked an eye three years ago when Warner drove Caudell Senior into the wall at Darlington and killed him. He'd be damned if he was going to let the fucker do the same to him. "Tell him to keep off my ass, or he won't finish a race in one piece all season."

"Listen here, C.J. That kind of talk won't be tolerated. You can't threaten another driver and get away with it."

Dell narrowed his blue eyes, adopting the one thing he had in common with his old man, a steely-eyed look that could cut a man to shreds. "It's not a threat. It's a promise."

The room was silent except for the drone of high-performance engines on the track. Dell stared down the AARA officials, hating that he was in the official hauler instead of on the track.

"You took out six other drivers, including Warner, C.J."

"They were all start and parks anyway."

"Yeah, they were, but those kind of teams can't afford to lose cars and stay in business. And AARA can't afford to lose them. You can't continue to drive the way you do. You're reckless, C.J. You're out of control."

"What about Warner?"

"What about him?"

Old doubts began to creep in, sapping his confidence. "He hit me first." Dell tried his best to keep from sounding like a petulant child complaining about the schoolyard bully, but that's what it sounded like, even to his own ears. Shit.

"Pack up your hauler and leave, C.J. Go back to Charlotte. We'll deal with Warner. When we make our decision, we'll notify your team owner."

Dell shrugged and pushed away from the wall. "Yeah, you do that," he mumbled as he shut the door behind him.

He pasted on a happy-go-lucky face for the reporters waiting for him. After a few minutes smiling, as if all was well, and plugging his sponsor, he headed for his motor home. He should help the crew load the hauler, but he didn't want to face them yet. Months of work to get ready for the first race of the season, the Daytona 500, and they'd be halfway home before the race was over.

Inside, he shed the fire suit, tossed it in a heap in the corner of his bedroom and pulled on his favorite jeans and T-shirt. He grabbed a beer from the refrigerator and stretched out on the built-in couch. The race was nothing more than the buzzing of a giant mosquito in the well-insulated motor coach. Dell shut it out as he'd learned to do before he could walk. Hell, he took his first steps on the track at

Talladega, twenty-six odd years ago. This was home, even more so than his big new house on Lake Norman.

He brought the bottle to his lips and savored the slide of cool liquid down his throat. It quenched his thirst, but did nothing to wash away the bitter taste in his mouth. For perhaps the millionth time, he asked himself what he was doing. Three years after that son-of-a-bitch Warner drove Caudell Senior into the wall, and here he was, still trying to prove his father wrong.

He closed his eyes and their last conversation played over in his mind. Darlington. Summer. Heat so hot, your lungs protested every breath. The noise of the garage. Engines revving. Air wrenches. Voices raised to be heard over the din. Caudell summoned his son, and even though Dell was certain what he was going to say, he went anyway. They stepped outside in the blazing sun.

"You'll never get anywhere in this business, C.J. You drive like an old lady out for a Sunday picnic. Hell, son – you should get out before you get killed." It was an old argument, one as far as Dell was concerned, was pure bullshit.

"I finished ahead of you in Phoenix," Dell argued. "Half the pack finished ahead of you."

"You got lucky, that's all. It won't happen again. Take some lessons from Richard Warner. That kid can drive."

Dell flinched at the mention of Dickey Warner. They were only a few months apart in age, Dickey being the younger of the two, but there was no love lost between them. They'd come up through the ranks, competing against each other since they were teenagers. It figured Caudell would approve of Warner's driving – if their cars didn't have different numbers and paint schemes, you wouldn't be able to tell the drivers apart on the track. They both drove like idiots.

Dell gritted his teeth and let his father finish his tirade. "If you think these drivers are going to let a wet-behind-the-ears pup like you run with them, you've got another think coming. Stick with trucks, or better yet, go-carts. You aren't cut out for this business."

"That's what you think, old man. You're just jealous because your racing days are almost over. You can't stand to see anyone else replace the great Caudell Wayne – especially your own son." He stood toe-to-toe and eye-to-eye with his father, determined not to let him see how badly the words cut him. "Well, hear this. I earned my ride, and I did it without your help." He ignored his dad's derisive snort. "I'll still be racing when you're dead and buried, and you know what? You know who they're going to be talking about then? Me. Dell Wayne. I'm twice the driver you are. You still drive like granddad taught you, like the revenuers are on your ass. It's a new sport, old man. It's passing you by. You're not on the lead lap anymore. Got that? The cars are different. The tracks are different. It's called technology. Progress." He jabbed a finger in the center of his father's chest to emphasize his point. "You're on your way out. We'll see who the best driver is. I'll wave to you from Victory Lane."

Dell sat up and drained the rest of the beer. "Shit." He ran a hand over his face, wiping away the memory and the tears that threatened. Goddamned hardheaded bastard. He's the one who should have quit while he was ahead. Instead, he raced Darlington like an idiot, allowed Dickhead Warner to force him into taking evasive measures, and did exactly what he warned Dell of, he got himself killed. Run into a concrete barrier going a hundred and sixty miles an hour. Stupid fucker.

Dell still had the trophy. It was currently doubling as a fire hydrant in front of the biggest goddamned doghouse in Iredell County. And as soon as he got himself some dogs, he was going to let them piss all over it.

The door opened, and Dell glanced up to see his friend and crew chief, Ray Mallard step in. "You okay, Dell?"

"Yeah," he sighed and stood. "Are we ready to go?"

"The hauler will be loaded in a few minutes. I thought we could get a headstart."

"Yeah. Yeah, sounds good. Let's get out of here."

Dell grabbed another beer and settled into the passenger seat. Neither man spoke until they navigated through the tunnel beneath the track and were on the freeway headed north.

"Want to talk about it?" Ray asked.

"Nothing to talk about. The bastard went after me on purpose, so I returned the favor."

"Look, Dell. We've been friends for a long time, but I have to tell you, the crew isn't happy. They want to win."

"We win our share."

"Yeah, but you either win or you wreck. There's never an in-between. If you'd converted a few of those DNFs last year into decent finishes, we would have made the Chase at the end of the season. As it was, you spent the last few races driving around in circles for no reason."

"The sponsor got exposure."

"They'd rather see their car in Victory Lane."

Dell shrugged. "We'll get them there enough to make them happy."

"What did the officials say?"

"The usual," he hedged. "It'll blow over. It always does."

"How long do you think AARA is going to let you keep driving like your car is your own personal rocketship to hell?"

"As long as I keep showing up to drive, they're going to let me."

"What about Anderson?"

Dell closed his eyes and considered the fallout from today in terms of the team owner. Virgil Anderson was a friend. When Dell was young and green, Virgil offered him a ride when no one else would. He was the only team owner who ignored the opinion of the mighty Caudell Senior who told everyone within hearing distance his son wasn't ready to drive in the Cup series. No, Virgil wouldn't toss Dell out now, not after he'd proved himself on the track these last four years.

"He'll come around. I've got my share of trophies in the case."

"I hope you're right."

ᘒᘒ

The phone call wasn't unexpected, but he wished to hell, it hadn't come at seven in the morning. The AARA officials must have burned the midnight oil in order to deliver their slap on the hand this early.

Dell parked in the slot with his name on it and pocketed his keys.

"Who won yesterday?" he asked as he passed the reception desk. Penny Anderson, Virgil's wife, was more reliable than ESPN.

"Randy," she said. She pointed a finger at the pedestal beside the desk where the most recent trophy held sway until replaced by another.

Dell's stomach clenched. Randy Cox was a good driver, and bringing home the trophy for the Daytona 500 was big, even for a team the size of Anderson Racing. He pasted on his I'm-a-team-player face and responded. "Hey, that's great. What does that make for Cox? Five?"

"Six. You forgot Fontana last year."

"Yeah, I keep forgetting that one." He and his wrecked car were almost to New Mexico by the time the race was over.

"You okay, Dell?" The genuine concern in her voice grated. Why did everyone keep asking him that?

"Fine." *Just fucking fine.*

He knocked on Virgil's door, entering without waiting for an invitation. The phone call had been invitation enough. "You wanted to see me?"

"Have a seat, Dell."

Dell settled into one of the plush leather visitor chairs and crossed one ankle over his knee. "So, how much is the fine this time?"

"No fine." Dell raised an eyebrow. No fine? That couldn't be good.

"What then?"

"AARA has suspended you for the next three races."

Dell jerked to his feet. "What the...? Suspended?" He paced to the door and turned. "What about Warner? What did they do to him?"

"That's not my concern, or yours."

"The hell it isn't. They're just going to let him get away with it? I don't fucking believe this."

"Sit down, Dell."

Dell glared at Virgil, unable or unwilling to believe what was happening.

"Sit down, son."

Dell returned to his chair and sat with his elbows braced on his thighs. "There's more?"

"Look, Dell... you know I think of you as a son. Your daddy was a hard man, but he was a friend. I hate to see you doing this to yourself. Ever since he hit the wall, you've changed. You aren't the driver you were when I took you on. Caudell was an idiot when it came to you. He loved you too goddamned much, I guess. He didn't want you to race."

Dell forced his neck muscles to cooperate and raised his head so he could look Virgil in the face. "What are you talking about?"

"I'm trying to tell you something – something important. Caudell and I were friends up until I gave you a ride. He never spoke to me again after I took you on, except to tell me he'd kill me if anything happened to you. I believed him. The man worshipped the ground you walked on."

Dell's laugh was without humor. "Let's suppose for a minute any of this preposterous story is true. Why did you give me a ride?"

"Because you're the best damned driver I've ever seen. Or you were. Look...Dell. I hate to do this, but I owe Caudell this much. I made him a promise, and I aim to honor it. I'm taking your ride. You're done, son."

Dell sat up. "I don't believe this. You tell me I'm the best, and in the next breath, you take my ride? What the hell?"

"I'm doing it for your own good, Dell. I promised your daddy I'd make sure you were safe. It was easy enough when you were driving like the pro you are, but ever since Caudell died, you've been driving like a madman. That's what the other drivers call you, behind your back. Madman. It's not a name I would have ever associated with Dell Wayne, but it fits the new you. You're a danger to yourself, and to the other drivers."

"You're shittin' me."

"No, Dell, I'm not. Your sponsor threatened to pull their support if AARA suspended you. They'll continue to sponsor the car, but they want another driver." He pushed a piece of paper across his desk to Dell. "It's all there in black and white. AARA will ban you from the track if you ever do anything like that again."

Dell studied the decree handed down from AARA.

"Take some time off, Dell. Get a grip on whatever it is that compels you to be a madman on the track. If you get it together, come see me. I'd like to see you back in the 21 car."

Chapter Two

Carolina eyed her senior crew chief over the desk. What to tell him? Somehow, telling him if they didn't start winning races, he and everyone else would be out of a job, sooner rather than later, didn't seem like a good idea. She needed to instill confidence, not fear. She needed to set a positive example.

"What happened on Sunday?" she asked.

Russell shrugged his shoulders and cast his eyes anywhere but at her. Damn. Russell was almost as old as her father, and one of his best friends. Answering to Stewart Hawkins twenty-three-year-old daughter wasn't something he accepted easily.

"Look, Russell. Whether you like it or not, I'm in charge now. Daddy's gone, and he isn't coming back. I own Hawkins Racing now, and I'm going to run it, so get used to it."

Russell fidgeted in his chair and Caro fought the urge to roll her eyes at him. This was all her father's fault. If he'd let her be a part of the business for the last few years, all this proving herself stuff would be behind her now. "Was it the car or the driver? How did the engine perform?"

She'd already read all the stats on the engine and knew it wasn't the problem, but she wanted to hear Russell's take on the race. Would he come to the same conclusion or would he place the blame somewhere else?

"The car was fine. It qualified well, and had the power to win."

She was relieved to hear him say what she already knew. "So?" she prompted.

"I hate to place blame, but in this case, I'd say the driver was at fault. Wilson doesn't have what it takes to run with the big boys, not yet anyway."

"He is young," she agreed.

"There are drivers younger than him winnin' Cup races."

"True." Caro tapped her pencil on the desk blotter. "What do you suggest?"

"We need a driver who's got the ba..., I mean, the guts to go up against the pack. Someone who won't back down from a challenge. Wilson lets the seasoned drivers push him around. Someone cuts him off, he just moves back a position and lets 'em go."

"He's not aggressive enough," she surmised.

"I guess you could say that. He does fine in qualifying and practice runs. There's nobody on the track to intimidate him – it's just him against the clock. He's green, but if you don't stand up for yourself during the race, they're gonna eat you alive."

"Hmm..." Caro leaned back and thought over what Russell was saying. He could be right. She'd seen it before. Racecar drivers had a pack mentality. If you showed weakness of any kind, the alpha males would single you out, do their best to toughen you up, and if you didn't come up to snuff, they'd push you out of the pack. "We need an alpha driver. A seasoned pro no one will mess with." She pinned Russell with a look. "Is that what you're saying?"

Russell nodded his balding head. "Yes, ma'am. That's exactly what I'm sayin'."

"Well, that does present a problem, doesn't it? Where are we going to get a driver in the middle of the season?"

Russell twisted his ancient baseball cap in his hands. "I don't know, Caro. I just don't know. Now, your daddy, God rest his soul, he would've whipped the kid into shape – "

"Thank you, Russell, for pointing that out. However, my father isn't here anymore. I'm in charge and I'll figure out something – preferably something that doesn't involve whipping."

Russell apologized for overstepping and exited, hat in hand, leaving Caro alone in the small office. She peered out the window overlooking the darkened garage. Everyone was gone at this hour, home to families and softball practices, and all those other things people did when they had a life.

Ever since she started looking more woman and less little girl, her dad saw to it she was kept as far from the garage and the tracks as possible. That meant boarding schools where they'd never heard of AARA, and served tea in china cups. Stewart Hawkins believed it would keep his daughter away from racing, teach her about the finer things in life, things he knew nothing about. But he didn't know anything about his daughter either.

Caro stared at the pristine garage. It was miles away from the greasy, disorganized shop she'd hung around instead of drinking tea, and though it was only a short walk from her dorm, it was light years away in every other aspect. The old mechanic who owned the place hadn't wanted her there anymore than her father would have, but she'd gradually worn him down. Her questions and book knowledge of automobiles eventually won him over and he'd taught her what he could about internal combustion engines and how to work on them.

She'd been complimented more than once at school about her well-manicured fingernails, but no one knew she kept them polished to cover the grease stains underneath, which no amount of scrubbing could erase.

Another four years away, studying engineering and every subject related to racing, and she'd come back to North Carolina, ready to be a part of Hawkins Racing. A year later, and she was running the family business, but not because Stewart Hawkins saw the error of his ways. No, up until a massive heart attack cut short his life, he kept Caro "in her place" – sitting around, pretending to be a lady.

"Well, Daddy," she said. "I'm Hawkins Racing now, and we're going to do it my way."

Caro turned her back to the empty garage and stared at the financial reports on her desk. There was only one driver with the ability to turn things around for Hawkins Racing, but he also had the ability to drive the final nail in their coffin.

She'd known Dell Wayne her entire life. They'd ridden their bicycles around the infields together, and painted used lug nuts for checkers on the old game board they'd found in her daddy's hauler. Dell was different then. He was happy. Fun to be around.

She hadn't seen or spoken to him in years, but she followed his career. Racing was as much in his blood as it was hers. About the time she'd gone off to boarding school, Dell took to racing anything with wheels. He was good. Really good. All the track announcers talked about him as the heir apparent to his father's legacy. Some speculated he would surpass his father in wins and records.

But that was in the past. Before Caudell Senior wrecked at Darlington.

They called him Madman now, and with good reason.

Caro sat at her desk, twirling a pencil between her fingers. Dell was the only Cup driver who didn't have a ride, and the reason for that was the same reason she shouldn't even consider offering him her ride. She leaned her head against the high back of the new ergonomic chair she got to replace her dad's old, worn out one, and closed her eyes. Which was worse? Taking a chance on Jeff Wilson manning up on the track and becoming the driver they needed before Hawkins Racing ran out of money? Or taking a chance on Dell Wayne? Dell either wrecked or won. The winning part was what they needed, the wrecking – not so much. Too many of those, and Hawkins Racing would redline for good.

Dell had one more week on his suspension. If someone else had offered him a ride, they were keeping it mighty quiet – not an easy thing to do in the small world of professional stock car racing. Everyone knew everyone else's business. Just like their moonshining forefathers knew what all their neighbors and competitors were doing. Not much had changed since driving moved from necessity to sport.

Caro contemplated her situation. It was possible Dell was off the market. There were a few people in the business who could keep their mouths shut. She stashed the grim reports in her briefcase, flicked the light switch, and shut the door behind her. With nothing more than the illuminated exit signs to light her way, she made her way to the front of the building, past trophy cases gleaming with evidence of past glories.

Caro ran her fingertips over the hood of the display car, standing sentinel in the middle of the lobby – a testament to the heyday of Hawkins Racing, when nearly every car on the circuit ran a Hawkins engine. The garage was busy around the clock to keep up with the demand, as well as field their own drivers. Plural. When she left for boarding school, Hawkins Racing ran three cars in the Cup Series, and twice that many in the lower series.

It was time for new trophies and past time to replace the relics of days gone by with something new. Something that would represent the future of Hawkins Racing.

A warm breeze caressed her cheek and lifted the single strand of hair dangling from her sleek updo as she turned to lock the front door. No use dwelling on it any longer. When it came to options, no matter how she tried to convince herself otherwise, there was only one thing she could do.

❧❧

She didn't know what she expected, but this wasn't it. Even though she'd seen Dell on TV dozens, hundreds of times since he'd grown up, nothing could prepare her for the sight of him in person. He stood framed in the doorway, lit from a light somewhere in the cavern of his house, while Caro stood on the darkened porch, staring. Dell Wayne. All grown up. And scowling.

"Hello, Dell," she said.

"Carolina?" His scowl turned to a smile as recognition dawned.

"How have you been?" she asked.

"Fine," he said stepping back and sweeping his arm in invitation. "Come in, come in."

Caro stepped past him into the marbled entryway. The door closed behind her with a solid thunk, and she turned to her host.

"My, my. Who would have thought little Carolina Hawkins would turn out like…" He eyed her up and down. "This." He shook his head. "It's good to see you, Caro."

"It's good to see you too, Dell."

Silence descended as Dell stood smiling and staring at her as if he couldn't believe his eyes. "Oh, hey…come in." He led the way and Caro followed him to the source of the light – a large den furnished with comfortable, overstuffed brown leather furniture and a flat-screen TV that would rival the giant HDTV at Charlotte Motor Speedway.

"Have a seat. Can I get you anything? Beer, soda, water?"

"No, thanks," Caro said as she sank to the edge of the long sofa. "I'm good." In better lighting, Dell was even more striking than he was on TV. He'd been a cute kid, but back then, she hadn't given a thought to the man he would become. He was tall for a driver. Nearly six feet, she guessed. His body was lean, and the way he moved suggested a well-toned musculature that obeyed his every command. His dark hair was in need of a trim, but on him, it looked good. The laughing blue eyes she remembered were still startlingly clear, but now there was something about them, a depth that wasn't there when he was younger. She supposed it went along with growing up.

Dell wasn't a kid anymore. He was a man. A good-looking one with boatloads of money and he drove racecars. Women probably showed up on his doorstep every day, offering him...anything he wanted. Caro swallowed hard as she thought about the things she might be inclined to offer him if things were different. If she weren't here to offer him a job.

Dell flopped into the chair across from her and was almost swallowed up by the billowing cushions. "Wow," he said. "I can't believe you're here. I mean... in my house. After all these years."

"Well..."

"Hey," he sat forward and his smile vanished. "I'm sorry about your dad. He was a great guy."

"Thanks. He liked you too."

Dell's smile returned. "Maybe. I seem to recall him threatening to paddle my butt a time or two."

A little of the anxiety that tightened her shoulders slipped away and she smiled at the memory. This was familiar territory. Between them, they shared thousands of memories. "Yes, but you always talked him out of it, even when you deserved it."

"I did." Dell seemed to focus on something only he could see. His tone turned somber. "Those were good times."

"They were. I loved every minute of being at the tracks. I loved the giant campground, the smell of barbecue grills and the constant roar of engines. It was great place to be a kid."

"We had fun."

Neither spoke for a moment, lost in the past. Caro broke the silence. "I'm sorry about your dad. I was away...at school."

Dell sat back and the chair engulfed him again. "Don't worry about it." He dismissed her concern with a wave of his hand and the gravel in his voice.

"It must have been hard on you."

"So, Caro, why did you come here tonight?"

Chapter Three

Caro accepted the change of subject. Dell and his dad were at odds more than they'd ever agreed. Dell wanted to race, and Caudell didn't want him to. Dell did it anyway.

"I heard you lost your ride."

"Old news, Caro."

"Do you have any offers?"

"Nope. There isn't much call for a Cup driver after the season starts, unless…"

"Someone gets injured, or dies," she finished for him.

"Exactly."

"I'm running Hawkins Racing now. I need a Cup driver. Someone the other drivers will respect. Someone who can win races."

Dell studied her from his plush leather cocoon. She hadn't expected him to jump for joy, but she did hope he'd say something. His silence, this scrutiny from those blue eyes chipped away at the fragile wall of confidence she'd pinned her hopes on.

"What are you saying?" he asked – at last.

Air rushed back into her lungs. She tried to hide her relief behind what she hoped was an I-know-what-I'm-doing expression and plunged on. At least he was listening, instead of laughing his head off. She couldn't think of many drivers who would listen to a word she said. As far as most were concerned, she had two strikes against her: first – she was a woman: second – she was young. Too young, and too female to run a race team. She gulped in fresh air and laid her offer on the line.

"I want you to drive for me. For Hawkins Racing."

No laughter. Not even a hint of amusement. Dell studied her some more and she did her best to keep still while every cell in her body squirmed.

"What about Jeff Wilson?" he asked.

A legitimate question. "You've seen him drive. He doesn't have the confidence to compete at this level."

"So, he's going to lose his ride?"

"If I can find someone to replace him, I'll move him down to a lower series or keep him on as a spotter. I'm hoping he can learn from you. He needs a mentor."

"You've never seen me drive."

"What makes you think that?"

"You were away at school. Television doesn't count. It's not the same as seeing it in person."

"I saw you win at Pocono, what was it? Four years ago? I saw your fifth-place finish at Watkin's Glen. And your DNF at Pocono last year."

"How? I can't imagine your dad was happy about you being there."

"He didn't know. I bought a ticket and sat in the stands. A friend loaned me a car. As long as I brought it back with a full tank of gas and no dents, I was free to use it whenever I wanted to. I couldn't see all the races up north, but I made it to a few. Enough to know you're a good driver."

"You don't know anything, Caro."

"You're turning me down?"

"No. I didn't say that."

Caro tried to repair her confidence that slipped several notches when she thought he was going to turn her down. She seized on his lack of refusal, deciding to treat it as a victory for her. If she acted like he'd accepted, he'd have to go along, or clearly state otherwise. She was counting on the former. "Good. Then...as soon as your suspension is over, I want you in the garage. I'll have the lawyers draw up a contract for you to sign, and I'll have a fire suit made up for you. Is there anything else you need?"

"Money?"

Caro hesitated. There was no avoiding the subject. She held the top of her purse in a white-knuckled grip and looked him in the eye. There wasn't any way to gloss this part over, and she couldn't bulldoze her way through it either. Her confidence slipped another notch. "I can't match what you were making. I can't even come close."

"What did you have in mind?"

Negotiate. He wanted to negotiate. She could do this. Really, she could.

"I was hoping you would take a percentage of the winnings, and of course, the sponsor will be generous."

One strong eyebrow lifted in tandem with one corner of his mouth. Caro braced herself for the belly laugh she'd been expecting ever since she voiced her proposal. "Meaning all the barbeque I can eat?"

"It's a bit more than that, but yes, all you can eat. I know Marvin's Barbeque Pit is a step down for you, but they're good people."

"They know their barbeque too," he agreed. "It's not like I need the money."

Her heart rate sped up and her confidence level accompanied it. No, Dell Wayne didn't need money. He'd won enough races on his own to ensure a more than comfortable lifestyle for some time to come. Add Caudell Senior's estate to the bottom line, and Dell could sit on his ass for the rest of his life. She was counting on that being the antithesis of what he wanted.

"But you need a ride," she stated.

"I need a ride, and you need a driver."

"Good." Relief poured through her and she loosened her grip on her purse. "I'll call you when the contract is ready."

❧

Dell closed the door behind her and watched through the sidelight as Caro walked to her car. Who would have thought little Carolina Hawkins would grow up to look like that? When he opened the door and saw her standing on his porch, he thought he was hallucinating. He'd heard she was back, and running Hawkins Racing, but he hadn't seen her until tonight.

Damn. Now he understood some of the bawdy comments he'd heard around the garage. Caro had always been pretty, but she'd also been a tomboy – smudged with dirt and grease. She couldn't go five minutes without getting dirty.

She wasn't dirty tonight. Nope. Her classy clothes were spotless with that crisp, don't-even-try-to-guess-how-much-I-cost look about them. Her father had been right to send her away. She turned into a first-class lady, and a beautiful one too. When her taillights were out of sight, he shook his head and returned to the den and the six-pack he'd been working his way through when she came calling.

He opened another bottle and downed half in one long pull. The cold liquid did nothing to ease the ache in his groin or erase the image of Caro Hawkins' shapely ass from his memory. The skinny tomboy wasn't skinny anymore. She'd developed more curves than the track at Sonoma, and those legs... what he wouldn't give to see the full straightaway of those. Preferably wrapped around his hips, or spread on his bed. Then there was the thing she did with her hair. Some sort of tight coil intended to ward off the entire male population, but having the opposite effect. On Caro, it looked utterly feminine and screamed a challenge no human with a y chromosome could ignore. He had a sneaking suspicion if you got the hair to unwind, the prim little skirt she was wearing, and the silk blouse would disappear faster than a pit stop.

But he wasn't going to be the one to make it happen. For some reason he couldn't fathom, he agreed to drive for her. She was the boss, and Dell had never screwed an employer, and he sure as hell wasn't going to start now. No matter what.

Besides, this was Caro Hawkins. He'd raced her Big Wheel-to-Big Wheel when they were kids. He wondered if she still liked peanut butter and banana sandwiches and RC Cola or if her tastes were more sophisticated now, like the way she dressed. There wasn't much about the new Caro Hawkins that resembled the one he remembered, except those eyes, and those lips. He'd been barely old enough to start noticing those things when her dad sent her away.

He'd hated like hell for her to go, but seeing the way she turned out, it was a good thing. No one in the Hawkins' garage would have gotten a damned thing done with her around. Throwing all that brewing estrogen into a garage full of testosterone would have ignited one hell of a blaze. He wasn't entirely sure it wouldn't now. Sure, she was older, and presumably able to rein in her sexuality when need be, and now that she was the boss, even more off limits than when she was the boss' daughter.

That was crap. Everything about her was feminine, from her womanly curves to the intelligence in her eyes. Her presence would disrupt a garage full of eunuchs.

21

What the hell was he thinking? Did he want a ride that bad? He drained the rest of his beer and let his head drop against the back. No. He didn't want a ride that bad – he needed a ride that bad. The only time he was able to forget was when he was driving – fast. The faster, the better.

The AARA official accused him of being suicidal on the track. They didn't have a clue what they were talking about. On the track was the only time he wasn't suicidal. Behind the wheel of a stock car, he didn't have time to think about anything but self-preservation. Get distracted for a fraction of a second, and it would be all over. That was enough to keep him focused on staying alive.

It was all the other times – like tonight – before Caro Hawkins showed up on his doorstep with her offer of salvation. Those were the times when his life was in danger – from himself. From his memories. Too much time alone with those memories messed with his head.

At least Caro had given him something else to think about tonight. His hand went to his fly and he wondered if she'd have this effect on him when he was driving. He'd never tried driving with a hard-on before. It would be a new experience. Dell laughed. At least it was something new to contemplate. Better than trying to solve the mysteries of the universe, or dwelling on a past he couldn't change or a future that didn't exist.

❧❧

Caro drove out of Dell Wayne's gated community and turned into the first strip-mall parking lot she came to. Parking underneath a light standard – safety first, even in this enclave of the extremely wealthy, she dropped her forehead to the steering wheel between her tightly clenched hands.

Holy cow. What had she done?

The racing world was going to have a field day with this. Hawkins Racing didn't need the kind of publicity Dell would generate – they only needed to win. And lord knew, she didn't need Dell Wayne. Want? That was something entirely different.

Caro pushed away from the steering wheel and peeled her fingers loose. A tap on her window had her almost jumping out of her skin. A uniformed officer peered at her, signaling with his index finger for her to roll the window down. She lowered the glass half an inch and asked to see his badge. Satisfied he was the real thing, she powered the window down the rest of the way.

"Yes?" she asked.

"Are you okay, ma'am?"

"I'm fine. I needed to..." stop shaking? "rest a minute," she said. "It's been a long day."

"You might want to switch off the engine, ma'am."

"Yes, good point." Caro turned the key and smiled back at the officer.

He asked a few more questions, and being convinced Caro was fine, he bid her a good evening and walked away. She waited until he drove off before she allowed herself to slump in her seat.

Caro took in a deep, calming breath. The first full one she'd taken since Dell opened his front door and she got her first, up close look at the adult version of the kid she'd known. The ratty T-shirt he wore should have been a turn-off, but the way the thin cotton stretched across those broad shoulders... and when he moved, it hinted at firm muscles everywhere else. It was hot. And those jeans that looked like they'd been washed a million times? Oh, dear lord. The denim was faded all over, but in just the right places – a white denim whammy to the gut. The man needed new jeans. Jeans that didn't draw attention to places she shouldn't be looking. Or thinking about.

It wasn't seemly for a boss to lust... look at an employee that way. Like he was the last hot biscuit in the pan, with butter and honey oozing all over it.

Caro swallowed hard and licked her lips. She wouldn't mind having a taste of Dell Wayne. Just one little lick. Maybe on his forearm. That would be safe enough. As long as she didn't stray to the crook of his elbow where the skin looked so... or his neck. Heaven forbid if she licked his neck. She'd have to get real close to do that. Bodies touching close. Close enough to feel what lay underneath that T-shirt and those jeans. And if that happened, one lick probably wouldn't be enough.

Tires screeched and an engine roared nearby. Caro's head snapped up, and so did reality. This was ridiculous, sitting in a parking lot, lusting after a man she couldn't have. He was her driver. Or he would be, as soon as she got his signature on a contract, and that couldn't come soon enough. She looked around, spied a Starbucks on the far end of the shopping center, and headed toward it.

She ordered a venti hot chocolate, extra whipped cream, and took a seat by the window. The chocolate went a long way to calming her nerves. She'd made the biggest business deal of her life, and arguably, one of the stupidest. What did she really know about Dell Wayne? He'd burst into the Cup series four years ago, touted as the up-and-coming driver by all the reporters. And then his father died.

Caro sipped the warm drink and tried not to dwell on the negative, though it was hard to ignore the facts. Dell had been suspended from AARA, and fired from Anderson Racing for a reason, and it wasn't because of his innovative driving. But even when Dell was living up to his nickname, Madman, there was something about the way he drove that hinted at the potential he'd once shown the world. Things rarely happened *to* Dell. Everything, even the crashes, appeared calculated, planned, instigated – by Dell himself.

She sighed, finished her drink and tossed it into the bin by the door on her way out. She had work to do. Contracts to draft, a sponsor to win over to her new driver, and a fire suit to order. Getting Dell into a fire suit was high priority. Then she'd only have to look at his face and his hands. Hands that didn't resemble the ones she remembered in the least. She groaned. She wouldn't think about his hands, or his long fingers, or how strong they had to be to control a racecar. Or what they would feel like on her skin. Rough. Competent. Hot.

Gloves. She needed to order gloves. And a helmet. With a visor.

Chapter Four

Whatever made her think a fire suit was a good idea? Caro eyed the man standing in her office in the brand new fire suit – complete with gloves. The red piping on black around the neckline and waistband accented his slim physique, and extended over his shoulders, down his arms and the length of his legs, drawing attention to his height. He flexed his fingers in the buttery leather gloves and her lady parts tingled. She ignored the ill-timed feeling. After a week of seeing Dell almost every day, she had lots of experience ignoring those feelings.

"Too tight?" she asked.

"No. It's perfect. You did good, Caro."

"Your measurements were on file. I just told them what colors to use."

"Well, it's all good. I appreciate it. The ride, I mean. The suit too."

"You're welcome."

"All's square with the sponsor?" he asked.

Caro tapped her finger on the contract in front of her. "Yep. They came by and signed the new contract this morning. They even increased their involvement to include free ice cream if you win."

Dell's smile lit up the room, as well as a few other things. "Free ice cream. That's quite a commitment."

"Laugh if you will, but they're stocking up on ice cream."

His smile dimmed." They have that much confidence in my ability?"

"Of course they do. Why wouldn't they?"

"Oh, I don't know. Maybe because I've wrecked more than I've won in the last few years?"

"Or maybe they know what a good driver you are?"

"I'll try, Caro. That's all I can do."

"It's all I'm asking, Dell."

Caro admired his butt as he left her office. The man had it going on back there too. She frowned at his retreating backside. His body might be hot, but his personality ran hot and cold, and Caro never knew what to expect. One minute he was laughing about free ice cream, and the next, he was scowling and making excuses. He'd been moody as a kid, but never like this.

Caro tried to remember the adolescent Dell. As kids, they'd both had their disagreements with their dads. Caro's didn't want her in the garage, and Dell's didn't want him racing. Through it all, Dell was a happy kid – except those times he argued with his dad. Caudell Senior could be a hard man when he wanted to be, but Caro remembered him, if not fondly, respectfully. Like her dad, Caudell wanted what he believed was best for his only child, and it never occurred to him, said child might want something different. Both men were used to getting their way.

But Caro and Dell defied the odds, and look where they were. Well, look where Dell was. He was one of the best, while Caro still had a lot to prove. So why was Dell so quick to put down his abilities? Surely, he recognized his own talent.

When he was out of sight, Caro turned her attention to the new contracts. Once she announced Dell Wayne was going to drive for them, Caro received several sponsorship offers she had yet to consider. They weren't major offers, but a sponsor was a sponsor. Dell would be on the racetrack in a few days, and the more endorsements, the better. Caro was grateful her father's lawyer was still willing to look over the contracts: but as the new owner of the company, it was her duty to at least read through them. She looked forward to the day when she could afford to hire people to manage the office so she could spend more time in the garage. She understood the mechanical end of the business better than she did the business end.

Caro penned acceptance letters for two new sponsors. The contracts were small, but they were solid backing, just what she needed if Hawkins Racing was going to make it. Restoring the team to its former glory wasn't going to be easy, but Caro vowed to do it.

If she could get a positive cash flow going, and perfect the new engine design she'd been working on for the last few years, Hawkins Racing would, once again, be a respected name in auto racing.

A knock sounded on her door. Caro looked up, grateful for the interruption. Russell stuck his head in.

"The hauler is ready to go. You wanna come talk to the crew?"

Caro rose, dropping her pen on the desk. "Sure. I'll be right out." Russell nodded and shut the door behind him. Caro raised a hand to the back of her head and checked to make sure every strand was in place. The send-off was a race week tradition at Hawkins Racing, begun by her father, and continued by her. She grabbed her coveralls from the small closet behind her desk and slipped them on over her sand-colored linen slacks and cream-silk blouse.

The garage door was open, the hauler parked outside – ready to head out to Martinsville for the weekend's race. Caro smiled at the knot of mechanics, engineers and crew members standing beside the hauler. Most of them had been with Hawkins Racing for years and elected to remain so after her father's death. Some, she suspected, were hanging around to see how long it would take for her to do a face plant – something she had no intention of doing. Hawkins was once a respected name in racing, and Caro vowed to do everything in her power to make it one again.

✍✍

"Good afternoon," Caro greeted the gathering. Dell turned at the sound of her voice and surprise socked him in the gut. This was the Carolina Hawkins he remembered – except her hair was swept up in one of those fancy knots again, exposing the long, graceful lines of her neck. Gone was the pristine lady of the manor. In her place stood the grease-smeared hellion who had shown him how a carburetor worked when she was all of eight.

A chorus of male voices returned her greeting. Dell noted a few stepped forward to shake her hand, while the majority hung back. Dell moved to the back of the group and leaned his shoulders against the hauler, watching. Her Hawkins Racing coveralls were smeared with grease, but her small-boned hands were clean. Not a single golden strand of hair was out of place. The coveralls hid her womanly shape as his eyes traveled down the length of her legs to her feet. Red-tipped toes peeked from beneath the hem. Tiny beige straps crisscrossed her foot above her toes. He couldn't help but smile at the odd mix of class and sass.

She took a minute to recognize the newest member of the pit crew – a kid named Trent who came onboard to replace a tire carrier who did something to his ankle. Dell tuned the explanation out, content to watch her when she wasn't watching him.

As she moved from one man to the other, exchanging small talk and wishing them a safe trip and a win, Dell listened for anything that would tell him who this woman was. Was she the Caro he knew as a kid? Or was she Carolina, the princess in the ivory office?

She finally made her way to him. Dell pushed himself aside from the hauler and straightened.

"Dell," she offered her hand.

"Caro," he said as he folded her small hand in his bigger one. Her grip was firm and warm, not a hint of nerves, though he sensed some in her voice when she said his name.

"I hear you're driving with the crew."

"It's not far. Besides, I want to be there early." And he wanted to get to know them better. He'd only had a few hours with them this week. Most of his time had been spent playing the PR game – interviews, photo sessions, and making nice with his new sponsors. A good crew could make or break you, and their performance could be anywhere from lousy to outstanding, depending upon their opinion of the driver. If a few hours on the road with them could help win them over, he was willing to go along.

"I'll see you on Thursday, then." Dell raised an eyebrow in question.

"I like to be there for practice. There isn't much time to get the car as good as it can be," she said, as if that were her explanation. Before he could ask her what she meant, she moved to the front of the group and raised her hand above her head. All eyes turned her way and everyone grew quiet.

"Be careful," she said. "We're fortunate to have an experienced Cup driver on our team now, so let's give him our support. I think we have a winning team. I believe in each and every one of you." She waved her hand. "I'll see you on Thursday."

Dell accepted a ride with the crew chief. If he remembered right, Russell was a childhood friend of Stewart Hawkins, and part of Hawkins Racing from the beginning. If anyone knew Caro, Russell did.

"What do you think of the new owner?" he asked.

Russell didn't take his eyes off the road, and for the longest time, Dell didn't think the man was going to speak at all. When he did, Dell was almost sorry he'd asked.

"She needs to get married and have a bunch of kids, and get the hell out of the garage and the business. Ain't no place for a woman." Dell flinched, but chided himself for his stupidity. He should have known Russell would hold the same opinion as his friend, Caro's father.

"Stewart knew what he was about. Sent the girl away."

"She's not a girl anymore," Dell said.

Russell shook his head. "Anyone with eyes can see that. And trust me, you ain't the first to notice."

"I didn't think I was."

"The only mistake Stewart ever made was leavin' the business to that slip of a girl. I'm tellin' you, she ain't got no business runnin' a race team. She's gonna to drive it into the ground, you mark my words."

"I don't know – she seems to know what she's doing."

"She don't know shit. She hired you, didn't she?"

Dell didn't know what to say to that, so he turned his attention to the road. He had no idea if hiring him was a good thing for Hawkins Racing. He hadn't even considered that aspect when Caro offered him the ride. All he was thinking about was himself. He lived to drive and driving kept him alive. He couldn't let anything else enter into the equation. That's not how he worked.

They rode in silence for a while before Russell spoke up. "Your daddy was a good man." Dell held his tongue. How could he forget Russell knew his father too? "Had a good head on his shoulders. Hell of a good driver too."

Dell had heard it all before. Most of the racing world held the same opinion, and he'd given up on trying to change it. It seemed everyone but him knew the Caudell Wayne that Russell spoke of. Personally, Dell had never met that version of his father.

"He said you'd never make a decent Cup driver, and he was right. You got off to a good start, but it musta been beginner's luck. Always thought the other drivers cut you some slack your first season, because you were Caudell's son. After that, you had to earn your spot, and you ain't done it yet."

At last, something he could argue. "I've done alright."

"If you call wreckin' alright. I've seen demolition derbies with less damage than you do on a racetrack."

"They aren't all my fault."

"Don't matter whose fault it is, the result's the same. Scrap metal ain't a trophy."

Silence filled the truck cab again. Dell wasn't used to defending his driving. Ever since his last argument with his dad, he'd left the topic of his driving skill to the commentators, and done his best to ignore them at the same time. His avoidance skills weren't in question. They were trophy quality, all the way.

"How's the crew?" he asked.

"They know their stuff. Might not be the best in the business, but they're okay." Dell had worked with less skilled crews. "Biggest problem is, she's got some of 'em pussy-whipped. That darn fool woman comes in the garage wearin' those coveralls, tellin' 'em what to do." Dell turned his head so Russell wouldn't see him roll his eyes as the crew chief went off on another misogynist rant. "Woman don't know her place. I blame that on Stewart. He sent her away alright, but he sent her up north. Filled her head with all that liberal women's lib shit."

Dell picked up on the only part of Russell's tirade that was pertinent. "What does Caro tell them to do?"

"Everything from engine adjustments to bitchin' about keepin' the tools in order. I'm tellin' you, the woman don't know her place," he repeated.

Dell didn't know anything about women's lib, but he did know what century it was. "Does she know what she's talking about, with the engine adjustments?"

"Hell no! She's a woman."

"Are the mechanics taking her advice?" Getting useful information out of Russell was harder than finding gold in a coalmine.

"Some."

He'd done a bit of research on Hawkins Racing in the last week, and no one was arguing about the quality of their engines. "You're still building your own engines?"

"One of the few," Russell said with pride. A good engine builder could make a fortune building and selling to other teams, but as far as he knew, Hawkins wasn't selling to anyone else. He wondered why, but he wasn't going to ask Russell. He'd bet his next trophy the answer would place the blame on Caro.

Dell mulled that over. He wondered how much input Caro actually had when it came to the engines. Unlike Russell, he didn't dismiss her knowledge because of her gender. The Caro he remembered had a good, basic knowledge of a racecar when she was ten, and if she'd spent the last decade increasing her knowledge, she might know what she was talking about. He'd find out soon enough.

When Dell didn't respond, Russell continued. "I don't know why she brought you on, and I don't give a damn why you came. I suspect it had somethin' to do with the skirt in the office, but as much as I hate the idea of a woman in this business, I like that girl. I've known Carolina all her life, and so help me, if you hurt her…well, I'll kill you myself."

Dell turned to watch the landscape speed by and let a smile lift his lips. The old codger might have his backward ways when it came to women, but he was loyal to a fault.

"Point taken," he said.

≈≈≈

Dell drove the car into the stall allotted to Hawkins Racing and killed the engine. The practice run was one of the worst he'd ever had. The car had a shimmy on the right side and was so loose, he almost spun out on the first turn before he figured out how to control it through the others. He pulled his helmet off and climbed out of the car. The crew had the hood up and their heads together under it before his feet hit the floor.

A familiar voice caught his attention. "Chet, adjust the track bar. Raymond and Pete, see where the shimmy is coming from." Dell strolled around to the front of the car and looked under the hood. Today, her hair was in a high ponytail that brushed her right shoulder, partially obscuring her face. She was elbow-deep in the engine compartment.

"Hey, what's up?" he asked.

She answered without looking up. "Not much. Just checking something. We had a shimmy like you reported once before. Someone left a bolt out of the mounting block. It's a simple fix, if that's what's wrong." She pulled her arm out and stood, brushing a stray lock from her face with her forearm. "All present and accounted for. We'll have to look elsewhere."

"It felt like it was in the wheel," he said.

"Like I said, just checking all the possibilities."

"Got it," Chet called from under the car. "We'll have to change out the shock on this side, but then she's good to go."

Caro praised Chet and Pete for solving the problem so quickly and turned to go. Dell caught up with her before she reached the hauler. "Hey, wait up," he called.

She continued on, only stopping when she wrapped her hand around the door latch. "The car should be ready to go in a few minutes. See if you can get her back on the track as soon as possible."

"Will do, boss. I was wondering… would you like to get a burger with me tonight?"

"You go ahead without me, Dell. I've got a lot to do tonight." She opened the door, but stopped and turned half-around. "I'm sorry. Race weekends are busy for me. Maybe next week?" she asked.

Dell nodded. "Next week then."

He made a few more practice runs before calling it a day. He had a few hours to himself, a few hours too many. He caught a ride to the hotel and cleaned up before heading out to one of the local bars. With only qualifying tomorrow, and the race on Sunday, one beer wouldn't hurt.

The place was packed with race fans and Dell kept his baseball cap on, pulled low over his brow. He found a table in the corner and settled in. A waitress took his order and he put his feet up on the extra chair, leaning back with the bill of his cap pulled over his eyes. Conversation was lively all around him. Two couples occupied the table to his left; their conversation divided along gender lines. Dell tuned out the female talk about the best diapers and zeroed in on the men's conversation. He listened as they speculated on whether Everhart would finally win a race this season or go down as the driver with the longest losing streak in Cup history. Dell mentally cast his vote for the history books, but remained silent.

His meal arrived and he took his time, savoring the excellent burger. The table on his right emptied, only to be grabbed up again by a group of men with mouths as big as their beer bellies. Dell tried to tune them out, but he would have needed noise-proof headphones to do it. Between the four of them, they had an opinion on every aspect of racing, none of which were based on any version of reality Dell knew of. He finished his burger, signaled the waitress for his check and was about to leave when their conversation turned interesting.

"How about that Sadie Hawkins?" one of them asked as the rest guffawed and contributed more inappropriate comments about the woman.

"Heard she was shagging the crew chief," one said.

"That old man? Naw, I heard that's how she got Dell." another said. "I'll bet he's driving more than her car." They all laughed at the remark, adding a number of lewd comments that resulted in more laughter. Dell sat back and listened briefly. He didn't care what people said about him, hell, it had all been said a dozen times: but when it came to Caro, he didn't like what he was hearing. These people didn't know her. They just didn't want a woman invading what they perceived as their territory.

"Maybe he'll knock her up and send the little woman home where she belongs."

"If he doesn't, someone else will. I bet she spreads those legs of hers for anybody with a dick."

Dell had heard enough. He rose from his seat, removed his cap and held it tightly with both hands to keep from belting one, or all of them. Two steps brought him to their table.

"Excuse me," he said. Four faces turned to him. He waited until they recognized him and realized they'd been talking about his new boss and him. "I don't care what you say about me personally, but the lady in question doesn't deserve to be talked about that way. I'd appreciate you minding your own business."

Dell slipped his cap back on and left, congratulating himself on getting out before he did something that would get him suspended from racing – again. AARA frowned on drivers punching out the fans, though in Dell's opinion, the sport could use a few less fans like those.

.

Chapter Five

Caro gasped, but refused to look away. Everything had been going smooth, up until now. Now, all she could do was sit atop the war wagon and watch helplessly as her racecar spun down the track, sliding completely out of control through the narrow strip of grass between the track and the inside wall on turn three. When it came to a halt, it was facing backwards.

She closed her eyes and sent up a prayer that Dell was all right – even if he deserved to die for that last stunt. He'd passed the 28 car without incident. Why he slid in front of him like he did was beyond comprehension. Getting bumped and spun out was what he deserved.

"You okay?" Russell asked Dell.

Her headset crackled. Dell's voice met her ears. "I'm alive." Caro sighed in relief. "Car's okay, I think. Restarting now."

She watched in disbelief as Dell spun the car around in place, and roared back onto the track. He was several laps behind now, but he drove with the determination of someone defending his first place status.

"You've got grass in the grill. Bring it in," Russell ordered.

"Not yet. I'll pit with everyone else, unless we have another problem," Dell answered.

"What's with him?" Russell asked Caro. "Doesn't he know he's done for?"

"I don't know," Caro said. "He's lucky no one hit him on the spinout."

"Skill, not luck. He steered the car out of the way before he lost control in the grass."

"You think?"

"I know. He spun halfway down the back straightaway and into turn three and the caution flag never came out. That took skill."

Caro shrugged. Skill or no skill, Hawkins Racing wasn't going to get a win today, and they didn't garner any favors with the other drivers either. For the first time since she came up with the idea to hire Dell, she began to wonder if she made a mistake. The man could drive a racecar — no one would dispute that — except maybe Dell's father. She didn't know all the details, but she did know the two of them didn't see eye-to-eye when it came to racing.

Twenty laps later, and they were done. Dell lowered the net on the driver's side window and Caro let out a pent-up breath. He was alive. She was going to kill him.

The car was a total loss. They'd be lucky to salvage any part of it. As Dell climbed into the back of the ambulance — standard procedure following a crash — Caro mentally calculated what the loss of the car would do to their bottom line. The prognosis wasn't good. They'd have no choice but to use the backup car for next week's race in Arizona, and they'd have to work around the clock to build another one. That meant money out the door. Money they couldn't afford.

᠅

Dell cursed as he pulled himself up and out of the car. He managed to make up the laps he'd lost on the spinout, and was inching his way up on the lead lap when disaster struck. He couldn't say exactly what happened — someone ahead of him spun out, crashed into someone else, then all hell broke loose. He looked around at the carnage. At least a dozen cars were beyond driving, his included. This wasn't the way he wanted his first race with Hawkins to end, but some things couldn't be helped.

After being checked out at the track's medical center and pronounced sound, Dell made his way back to the hauler. Caro stood with her back to him, supervising the repacking of their equipment. Dell took a moment to admire the way she filled out her fire suit. She was a paradox, all business in her team gear, but the ponytail threaded through the loop in her cap made her look fragile, and feminine. Dell's palms itched to curl around the fall of hair and tug her against him. He'd never wanted to get his hands on an ass in a fire suit before, and he shouldn't be thinking about it now.

"Caro," he said. She turned to face him. Dell was so surprised at the genuine concern on her face, he wanted to hug her.

"Are you okay?" she asked.

"I'm fine. The car took most of the impact," he said, glancing at the heap of twisted metal the crew was getting ready to load into the top rack for the return trip.

"So it seems," she said. "Come with me." Dell followed her to the lounge at the front of the hauler where she evicted Russell, with instructions to leave them alone. Once Russell closed the door behind him, Caro turned to Dell. All her earlier concern for his physical being was gone from her face, replaced by red-hot anger.

"What were you doing out there?" she asked.

"Racing."

"Is that what you call it? Because if it is, you and I have a different definition of the term." Her hands were fisted on her hips and her ponytail swished from shoulder-to-shoulder as she paced the small lounge.

"Wrecks happen, Caro. You know that."

"Yes, they do, but you don't have to make them happen, Dell. This one was your fault. You were driving crazy." He opened his mouth to argue, but her raised hand stopped him. "Don't argue the point. I was there. I saw it all. You shouldn't have been trying to pass in that situation. It couldn't be done. And don't tell me your spotter didn't tell you the same thing, because he did." She was something to see, pacing the lounge like a caged animal, venting at him in that singsong voice of hers. Dell wiped the smile from his lips as she turned back in his direction.

"Can I say something?" he asked.

"No. You can't, Dell. I don't want to hear anything you have to say unless it's that you won't do it again." She stopped her pacing. Her shoulders rose and fell as she took a deep breath before she continued. "We're hauling home scrap metal, Dell. Scrap metal." Her voice rose an octave on the last two words. "We'll have to take the backup car to Phoenix, and God knows what you'll drive if something happens to that car during practice or qualifying. At this rate, we'll have to drag the show car out of retirement."

She paused, and Dell thought she might be expecting him to say something now, but he didn't have a clue what that might be. He'd done his job. He drove the car – and tried his best to be a contender.

"Well," she said. "What do you have to say for yourself?"

"Look, Caro, I did what you hired me to do. I drove the car. If you don't like the way I did it, then you should have hired someone else." Her cheeks turned pink and her lips turned white. Dell continued. "You knew what you were getting when you hired me. If you want a mouse behind the wheel, put Wilson back in the car. He won't wreck, but he won't win either. You said you wanted to win: well, that's what I was trying to do. The only way to win is to lead the pack, and to do that, you have to pass cars."

"I know that, Dell," she said. "I'm not stupid. I know you have to pass cars to win, but Dell, you took too many risks. It was only a matter of time before you wrecked."

"What are you so pissed about? I don't get you, Caro. Do you want me to race or not?"

"I want you to race, Dell. But I want you to listen to your spotter and your crew chief. This is a team sport, Dell. T.E.A.M. No I's in the word team." She poked a finger into the center of his chest. "Don't forget it."

He couldn't help it. He laughed. She was too damned cute in her fire suit, her face flushed with anger and that damned ponytail swinging like a pendulum, tempting him to grab it and yank her head back so he could kiss her. Whoa! He yanked his thoughts back instead. He shouldn't be thinking about kissing Caro Hawkins. Not now. Not ever. The conversation he overheard in the bar popped into his mind. Kissing Caro would be way out of line.

"What's so funny?"

Dell sobered. "Nothing," he said. "Look, I don't know what to tell you, Caro. I drive to win. I'm not going to sit back and let the other drivers decide where I finish. I'm the only one who gets to do that."

"What part of team sport do you not understand?"

"I understand what you're saying, but you have to understand too. I'll listen, but I'm the one driving the car. I'm the one who decides what risks to take. No one else."

Caro stood toe-to-toe with him for a long, silent moment. She stepped back. Her shoulders slumped and her body seemed to shrink. She dropped onto the sofa that took up one wall, and turned tired eyes on him. "Are you trying to kill yourself, Dell? Is that what this is all about for you? Is that why you drive the way you do?"

Dell froze as her words hit home. Was that what he was doing? No. No. He was only trying to win. He stood there, his gaze locked with hers as he considered her question. It was stupid. Completely off the wall, and so far off base he could never tell her the truth. He searched for words to counter with and found none. Instead, he strode to the door and stopped with his hand on the latch. "We'll win in Phoenix," he said. He pushed the door open and left, having said all that needed to be said.

చివ

Caro closed her eyes and focused on breathing. In. Out. Repeat. This wasn't working out the way she'd planned. She'd gone from a driver who the other drivers wouldn't let finish the race, to a driver who would either win or wreck – all on his own. She counted to ten before opening her eyes. She had no one to blame but herself. Hiring Dell was her idea. Admittedly, it might not have been the best one she'd ever come up with, but damnit, Dell Wayne could drive a racecar. The last three seasons, notwithstanding.

She needed to think, analyze. Find a way to fix this.

As she made her way through the pedestrian tunnel to her car, she considered her predicament. She hired Dell for a reason – not just because he was the only seasoned Cup driver available, and certainly not because he was hot in a fire suit. And lord knew, the man looked like sin in that suit. No, she hired Dell because she needed the driver he was during his first year in the Cup competition, not because of the driver he was today. That first year, she saw something unique in him. It was difficult to pinpoint the difference between his first season and all the rest, but there had been something special about Dell's driving that year. *Brilliant,* came to mind.

That's what it was. He'd been brilliant. Not overly aggressive, not a patsy for every bully on the track as Wilson had been, but consistent, and methodical in his pursuit of victory.

That's the driver she wanted. He was in there somewhere. She just had to find him and convince him to drive for her. *That* Dell Wayne would establish Hawkins Racing as a leader in the sport. There was only one problem – she needed to find the one she *wanted,* before the one she *had,* bankrupted her. And she didn't have a clue how to go about it.

$\approx$

It was his day off. Hawkins Racing didn't have the monster PR machine of some race teams, so his day off was actually a day off. No public appearances, no photo shoots, no interviews. Just time. Time to think. And the one thing on his mind was Caro Hawkins. Ever since she appeared on his doorstep, he'd spent way too much time thinking about her. Most of his thinking fell more in the realm of fantasy, but damn, he couldn't get her off his mind. She was a puzzle he wanted to solve. She was smart – always had been, but now she was educated smart. One week with the team and it was clear, Caro called the shots. The woman wasn't a figurehead owner. She knew racing. She knew racecars, and she wasn't afraid to get grease under her fingernails.

She single-handedly ran the office too. Not that he knew a damn thing about business, but running a race team was hard work. There were sponsors to appease, contracts, parts and supplies to order, not to mention personnel to manage and a payroll. Throw in all the AARA paperwork and there was enough work to keep an army busy. So, while he had a day off, Caro didn't.

He entered through the front office rather than the garage. One thing Caro didn't scrimp on was the crew. She employed engineers, technicians, engine builders, mechanics, and a half dozen other specialized people to build her cars. They didn't need him hanging around, getting in their way. Caro was another thing.

His footsteps echoed through the empty hallway. Man, he hated to see Hawkins Racing like this. When he was a kid, this place overflowed with people. He loved coming here with Caro, hanging out, basically getting in everyone's way. He'd stare at the trophies in the cases, and bug anyone who would take the time to talk to him, from the receptionist to the engine builders. Even Caro's dad. Stewart Hawkins always seemed to have time to say something nice to him, but he'd also threatened to tan his hide a few times. Dell smiled. Some of his best childhood memories were in this place, and most of them included Carolina.

"Hi," he said, pausing in the door to her office. He crossed his arms over his chest and leaned against the jamb. "How's it going?"

"I'm busy, Dell," she said without looking up from her work. "It's your day off – go away."

"I thought you could use some help." If he stayed home, he'd be thinking or drinking, and he didn't want to do either one. He'd rather sit on his ass and watch Caro work than spend another day alone.

"The only help I need is to be left alone."

Dell ignored her, taking a seat in one of the chairs in front of her desk. He picked up a stack of forms and thumbed through them. "I can do these," he said, holding up the standard parts orders awaiting approval.

Caro dropped her pen and sat back with a sigh. "Look, Dell. I hired you to drive. This," she swept her arm over her paper-covered desk, "is my job."

"I'm not saying it isn't, Caro, but I haven't got anything else to do today. Let me help you. I think I can manage to order parts without screwing up."

"Give me those," she put her hand out and wiggled her fingers. Dell laid the papers in her hand. She stacked them on the corner of her desk, out of his reach and shuffled through another stack. In a minute, she handed him a folder. "Here. These are the travel arrangements for Phoenix. Go in the other room and call the hotel, the airport shuttle service on this end, car rentals in Phoenix, and the helicopter charter for race day. It's all in the folder. If I've reserved it, verify it."

"Really? This is what you want me to do?"

"Really, Dell. It needs to be done. The car and your motor home leave tomorrow. The drivers need a place to stay when they arrive. The crew flies out Wednesday. They aren't going to be happy if there aren't hotel rooms for them, and I won't be happy if I have to sleep in your motor home at the track. And if I sleep in your motor home, you won't be. Does that clear things up for you?"

He'd noticed the dark circles under her eyes as soon as he walked in, but there was a strain in her voice too, as if she were holding on by a thread. Dell stood, folder in hand. "I'll be in the other room." It was a job for an intern, but Caro didn't even have one of those, so Dell sat at the desk intended for a secretary and opened the folder. A few phone calls wouldn't kill him.

More than once over the next hour, he wondered why he'd come. He'd sneak a peek at Caro, her head bent to her work and her shoulders slumped in fatigue and something would twist in his gut, then he'd go back to his phone calls.

She was working too hard. A race team was too much for any one person to run on their own. Even a team this size needed support personnel, people who did this kind of stuff – phone calls, reservations, ordering, scheduling appearances. Caro was trying to do it all on her own, and it was too much. On top of that, she was overseeing the garage as well. Hell, she was doing the work of at least half a dozen people, and Dell was going to find out why…as soon as he found her.

She'd disappeared while he was on the phone with the hotel where the pit crew would be staying in Arizona. He checked the other offices, ones he remembered being staffed back in the day. He found her in the garage, dressed in a pair of clean coveralls, arguing about an adjustment on the new fuel injection system now in use. Dell stood back and listened as she patiently, but firmly told the engineer what she wanted done, and why.

"He didn't have enough power to win last week, Charlie. If you make the adjustment, the engine will run better, and Dell might have a chance of winning in Phoenix."

"But, Ms. Hawkins –"

"Just do it, Charlie. I know what I'm talking about, and if it doesn't work, feel free to tell everyone it was my idea and you were only following orders."

"Yes, ma'am," he said.

"Good. I want this engine in the car and the test run done before we close up today. It has to be on the road tomorrow morning."

"Yes, ma'am, I'm aware of the time constraint."

Caro turned and saw him standing in the doorway. She raised one eyebrow at him.

Dell raised his hands in defense. "Hey, don't look at me. I'm all for anything that will squeeze more RPM out of an engine."

"You should be." She pushed past him and Dell moved a bit to let her pass. "I expect you to win in Phoenix."

"And I plan to. I always race to win," he said to her back as he followed her down the hall, watching her ponytail swish side-to-side. He was imagining it doing the same thing while she rode him, naked and flushed with passion.

"That's why I hired you."

"Will he make the adjustment?" Dell asked.

Caro stopped and turned to him. She fisted her hands on her hips and glared at him. "I have no idea. I could stand over him and watch, but there's no guarantee he wouldn't change it back as soon as

I left anyway, so you'll have to tell me after your practice runs. If he made the adjustment, you should have more power: if not, this engine will be identical to the one you ran last week. Even if you hadn't wrecked, you wouldn't have won. The car wasn't a winner, even on a short track. You've got to have more power to be competitive at Phoenix."

"I agree, but so you know, I race to win, even if I don't have a prayer."

"Well, if Charlie makes the adjustment I asked for, you'll have a prayer in Phoenix." She turned and walked away. Dell watched her backside sway side-to-side, wondering when he'd found coveralls so enticing. Never, was the answer. Of course, he'd never seen a pair filled out so nicely either. And he was dying to get his hands on her hair. He imagined some kind of secret pin hidden in there, and if a man were to find it, and pull…a cascade of silky blonde hair would come tumbling down….

He shook his head to clear it. Damn, he shouldn't be daydreaming about taking her hair down, or how those hips of hers would feel swaying against his, or how much fun it would be to peel the zipper down on those coveralls and kiss every inch of bared skin. He was pretty sure she wore them over her office clothes, but what if…? His little brain filled in the missing image of soft, pale skin, creamy breasts covered in something lacy and utterly feminine, something that matched the scrap of panties he'd have to slide his hand inside her coveralls to get to. Footsteps behind him snapped him out of his erotic, and completely inappropriate daydream.

Dell slipped into the first open door he found and leaned against the wall of the supply closet, closing his eyes and taking deep breaths. Caro had enough troubles without everyone in the place knowing her driver sported a hard-on for her. Pine cleaner and musty mop odor worked surprisingly well as an antidote to lust, and after a few minutes, Dell left the closet. He grabbed the travel folder Caro had given him and returned it to her office where she was, once again, in her prim Junior League outfit, hunched over her desk. Not that she wasn't sexy as hell in that get-up, but in those coveralls…

Dell caught a glimpse of them hanging on a coat rack in the corner and quickly shifted his gaze back to the woman behind the desk before his mind filled in the details again. He dropped the folder on her desk. "I confirmed everything."

"Thanks, Dell. I appreciate it."

"No problem, but is there a reason we don't have return plane tickets from Phoenix?"

"Oh!" she said. She pawed through another stack of papers and came up with another folder. "I forgot to tell you – we're going straight to Las Vegas from Phoenix. It will give us a few extra days to test the new car before practice begins for the race the following week. I've already made arrangements to get the new car there."

"What's to test?" he asked.

"Everything. There isn't a used part on it – all brand-spanking new."

"I'll look forward to it then."

She held out the folder in her hand. "Good. Then you won't mind confirming the reservations for Las Vegas."

Dell laughed as he took the folder. "Damn. I set myself up for that one, didn't I?"

"Yep, you did. Now go make phone calls. I have work to do here."

Chapter Six

Caro pretended to work as Dell left her office, folder in hand. Good lord! Why wouldn't he go away? Dell Wayne was a distraction she didn't need. It was bad enough he looked like sin in a fire suit and drove like a demon, but Dell in tight jeans and a T-shirt was more than any woman should have to deal with. If there were any doubt whether racecar drivers were athletes, one look at Dell dressed like that, and the naysayers would shut up. There wasn't an ounce of fat on the man, and his body-hugging clothes outlined every hard muscle.

Ever since the night she went to his home to offer him the job, inappropriate thoughts about peeling his clothes off and touching every sculpted muscle she found, ran through her mind on an endless loop that kept her on edge, and horny. Denial was pointless. Dell Wayne was too luscious, too damned hot for words. He made her want and need things she'd been successfully ignoring for a long time.

Caro stared blankly at the parts order in front of her. *Focus.* She needed to concentrate on her work. The garage couldn't function without parts and tools, and she was going to be on the road for at least the next two weeks.

Two weeks. On the road. With Dell. She gave a moment's consideration to booking a different hotel from the one where he would be staying, but this close to race day there wouldn't be a decent room available within a hundred miles of Phoenix. She'd simply have to keep her distance. Just because they would be in the same hotel didn't mean she had to see him any more than absolutely

44

necessary. Besides, he probably had women in every city on the circuit, and if he didn't, he wouldn't have any trouble finding one, or one hundred.

Moreover, she reminded herself, there were enough rumors going around about the state of their relationship, and there was no reason for her to add fuel to them by being seen with him outside the garage. She smirked as she signed the purchase order for the parts and moved on to the fuel and tire requisitions. Did people think she didn't hear the comments they made behind her back? As soon as she walked into her first owner's meeting, the rumors began to fly about whom she was sleeping with, and why. The world of professional stock car racing was the original old boys' club, and few had any place for a woman among them. Much less one her age.

She'd heard it all. She was too young. She didn't know cars or racing, or her head from a lug nut, even though she'd grown up on the racing circuit, hanging out in most of their garages at one time or another. She'd spent more time in the Hawkins Racing garage than in school in the days before her father sent her away. And as much as she hated those years away, they'd been a gift of sorts. They'd given her the freedom to learn everything she could about cars without her dad interfering. If she'd stayed, he would have controlled her access to the scientific and mechanical data she'd consumed like other underage kids did alcohol – and she'd done it all without her dad knowing a thing about it.

She was capable of providing knowledgeable input on the car's performance, and she had ideas that would make Hawkins engines run better. Convincing everyone else her ideas would work was going to be hard. And she'd never be able to do it if she were sleeping with her driver, or anyone else connected to racing in any way. From the AARA officials down to the pit crew, they were all off limits.

That meant her life was her work. Even if the company could afford the kind of staff it needed, Caro would still be here, putting in ridiculous hours by anyone's standards – because she had something to prove.

She needed to prove to AARA, to the fans, to her team and to herself her dad had been wrong. Maybe they were right to believe not just any woman could own and run a successful race team, but there was one woman who could. Caro Hawkins could. And she was going to prove it or die trying.

‹›〜

Dell throttled up as he came out of turn three, only to throttle back down again as he made it into turn four. With the backstretch ahead of him, he throttled up again and made another run at the lead. Only twenty laps to go, and victory was within his grasp. The adjustments Caro ordered to the fuel injection worked. After two hundred and forty-seven laps, the car still purred like a kitten, and ran like a cat with a pitbull chasing its ass.

"Nineteen to go," Caro's voice came through his headset. "We've made a good showing today," she said.

"We're not through yet," he countered. *Not by a longshot.* He'd be damned if he was settling for second when there was only one asshole between the checkered flag and him. It was all in the timing. He checked the fuel cell gauge and mentally calculated if he had enough to finish without pitting. He'd been getting good mileage all day – a benefit of Caro's adjustments. Tires were another thing. The new pavement here ate tires.

"Can somebody calculate the fuel for me?" he asked as he ticked another lap off. "I think I can make it if there isn't a caution, and if I don't have to make more than one run at the leader."

"Calculating now," Caro said. Dell waited. Finally, she came back on. "It's going to be close, Dell. If you had fresh tires…"

"I'm not pitting now. Five more laps and I'm making my move."

"You don't have to do that, Dell. Hold your position," Caro said.

"Behind you," Jeff warned from the spotter's roost above the press box. "Closing fast."

"Damnit," Dell said as he jerked the wheel to the right to cut off the car making a bid for his track position.

"You need new tires, Dell," Caro said.

"No new tires! I've got this," he said. He held off the challenge for five more laps. As he came out of turn four into the front stretch, he throttled up and rubbed bumpers with the lead car. "Come on, asshole, move over," he mumbled. The 15 car held his piece of track and Dell eased up against his bumper again. The lead car shot out ahead of him and Dell followed, kissing his bumper every chance he got. "Move it, lard ass," he said.

"Dell, what are you doing?"

Dell ignored the panic in her voice and nudged the lead car again. "You wanted to win, Caro, this is how it's done." He counted to ten and asked, "Laps?"

"Ten to go," Russell said.

Dell continued his assault on the lead car, mentally noting the laps. "Tell me when we get to three," he said to whomever was listening.

"Dell..." Dell ignored the warning tone and hit the lead car hard. The driver almost lost control, but managed to steer through it.

"Four," Russell said.

One more. Dell concentrated on his next move. He saw the checkered line painted on the pavement in the front stretch as Russell confirmed three laps to go. Dell bided his time. Split seconds. Through turn one. Turn two. Throttle up into the backstretch. He dropped down to the inside – mere inches and pressed the nose of his car against the bumper of the lead car, and pushed.

He saw the driver of the lead car try to steer his car back into the groove of the track and fail. As soon as the left side of his car cleared the right side of Dell's, Dell throttled up and passed him for the lead.

"Two," Russell said. "Hot damn, Dell!"

"Dell Wayne!" Caro yelled. "Are you crazy?"

Dell smiled. Damn straight he was. Crazy as a loon. "See you in Victory Lane, sweetheart."

◈

Caro pasted on a smile for the cameras and said all the right things, but inwardly she was seething. Five hundred laps of insane driving, and Dell acted like he'd won. Well, he had a trophy, and the purse would keep them in business for a while longer, but he'd lived up to his Madman nickname. It was nothing more than luck that had him standing in Victory Lane, swigging champagne and locking lips with the Miss Double-D Cup. And his last stunt? Totally unacceptable. Thank goodness it had been Stillwell he challenged. A lesser driver would have spun out and taken out half the cars on the lead lap.

By the time they made it back to the hauler, Caro was ready to explode. "What the hell were you doing?" she asked. "Is that what you call driving? How many did you shove out of your way today? Six...? More?" She paced the small lounge because she had too much pent-up anger to sit.

"Are you complaining?" Dell asked from his prone position on the sofa. "I won. We won," he amended. "Isn't that what you pay me for?"

She stopped her pacing and stared at him. God, he looked good, and she almost forgot why she was mad at him — then he ran his hands through his champagne-soaked hair and it all came back to her. "I'm paying you to drive, not to kill yourself."

The words dropped between them like a stone. Dell stilled. Like an animal sensing its prey, he swung his feet to the floor and stood. He towered over her, and even though he had to be exhausted, he looked ready to take on the world. Or one petite female team owner.

"You know what's killing me, Caro?" he asked as he closed the distance between them. Caro held her ground. He smelled of stale champagne and sweat, with a hint of burnt rubber thrown in. It should have been nauseating, but to Caro, it was the smell of victory, however won. She lifted her eyes to his as he slid one foot between her splayed ones and pressed his body into her personal space.

"Lord knows dying on the track would be easier than keeping my hands off you every day." He trailed one callused finger across her cheekbone, and down along her jaw to her chin to tilt her head back, telegraphing his next move with his firm touch. His gaze traveled from her lips to her eyes, giving her ample opportunity to say no, or to back away, but she couldn't.

His breath was hot against her face. His lips a mere inch from hers. "I'm going to die right here, Caro, if I don't kiss you."

Her heart leapt against her ribcage and her last grain of sanity gasped for her to run, but died from lack of oxygen as he pressed his lips to hers. His lips were warm and firm, and his kiss was sweet, almost tentative at first. In all her wild imaginings, she never believed Dell Wayne could be so gentle.

She moaned.

That did it. Dell's hold on decency slipped from his hands and he filled them with Caro instead. His hand beneath her chin moved to cup the back of her head while the other one found her sweet ass in her fire suit and pressed her softness against his hardness. She moaned again and he devoured her mouth. She tasted better than any champagne, and beneath the smell of burnt rubber and car exhaust clinging to her hair, was some flowery scent: beneath that, pure Carolina Hawkins.

Her lips were everything he dreamed they would be, and though he'd never been fire suit-to-fire suit with anyone before, he didn't want to let her go. She was the spark to his ignition and he went full throttle at her first moan. The little girl he'd played with as a child was all grown up and she had his lug nuts in a vise. He wanted her. And if the way she was kissing him back was any indication, she wanted him equally as much.

As he fumbled with the closure at the collar of her fire suit, he mentally checked off the steps to slipping her out of it altogether. Layers. Too many layers. The fire suit. Followed by the fireproof layer underneath, then…images of lacy undergarments flashed through his mind. Did she wear lace under all the protective gear? God, he hoped so.

He flicked her collar open and fumbled for the tab on her zipper, all without breaking the kiss. The zipper parted and his hand slid inside her suit. Undaunted by the Nomex undergarments, his fingers found skin. Hot, silky skin. He wrenched his lips from hers. Caro looked up, her eyes glazed with passion, her rosy lips wet and swollen. His gut clenched. He brushed his thumb across her stomach, watching her eyes for a cue to continue or stop. Everything in him screamed to take another lap, full throttle ahead, but this was Carolina Hawkins, and he wouldn't hurt her for anything, even for a victory lap.

"Touch me," she said.

"You're sure?" he asked.

She shrugged one shoulder, then the other, and the top of her fire suit hung from the waistband. "I'm sure," she said as she reached for the hem of the Nomex top and peeled it up to reveal his hands wrapped around her waist.

Dell swallowed hard at the sight of all that perfect alabaster skin. It was almost sacrilege to touch it with his callused hands, but he couldn't let go.

"A little help here, Dell," she said, breaking into his reverie.

"Yeah, let's get this off." He helped her lift it over her head and off without taking his eyes off the twin scraps of lace revealed in the process.

Before the Nomex hit the floor, his hands covered her breasts. The lace scratched his palms in contrast to the softness beneath. He squeezed both globes, and when she cried out, he groaned. "Beautiful, Caro. You are so fucking beautiful."

"My turn," she breathed. She fumbled with his collar. Dell helped her, and before he could decide if it were a good idea or not, his fire suit hung around his waist, and his Nomex undershirt joined hers on the floor. He was on fire, and there wasn't a suit in the world that could protect him from the flames licking his insides. He burned for this woman. Rational or not. Sane or not. It didn't matter.

Caro flattened her palms against his chest and Dell ignited. He framed her face between his hands and brought her lips up to his. Her hands explored. His lips conquered. Desperate to taste her, he used his thumbs to tilt her head back and trailed hot kisses down her neck, across her collarbone, and to the swell of her breasts above her bra.

Her skin smelled like roses and tasted like cream. He wanted more. He hooked a finger in the top of one lacy cup and jerked down. One sweet, ruby nipple popped free and he took it in his mouth. Caro moaned and one small hand cradled the back of his head, holding him to her while the other slipped around his waist. The bite of fingernails in his back sent a bolt of lightning to his groin.

He managed to free the other breast and shifted his attention to it, testing the weight of the first in his hand. Nothing had ever tasted, or felt, like this. Like his Carolina. Sweet. Hot. Magnificent. Perfection.

His head pounded, muffled by the roar of blood past his ears on its way south. Caro's fingers tightened in his hair and she tugged hard, dislodging him. He cursed and pulled her close with a hand at her back. He wasn't through. He'd never get enough of her unique taste.

"Dell," she said. The urgency in her tone and the sharp tug on the back of his skull got his attention. Blood still rushed past his ears, his scalp hurt, and the pounding – was coming from outside his skull. "Someone's at the door. We have to…"

"Get dressed, Caro," he finished for her. He grabbed the undershirts off the floor, handing her one as he jammed his arms into his suit.

"Be right there," he called to whomever was at the door. Thank God, whoever it was had the decency to knock instead of barging in. He zipped his suit and fisted his undershirt in his hand. He helped Caro fasten her collar back in place, and when she was all dressed, he dipped his head for one last kiss.

"We aren't through," he said, liking the flush on her cheeks and the way her lips looked after he tasted them. "Come in," he called.

Caro turned her back to the door, grabbed the race book from today's race and began to study it as the door opened. Russell stepped inside.

"The car passed inspection. We'll be loaded in a few minutes," he said.

"Thanks, Russell," she said without turning. "Is the chopper ready? Dell and I need to get back to the hotel so we can get cleaned up and on the road."

"Chopper's waiting for you. I've got a cart outside to take you to it."

Dell moved to the door. "Thanks, Russell. We'll be right there."

Russell glanced from Dell to Caro and back again to the undershirt fisted in Dell's hand. He moved to the door. "Okay, then."

Dell closed and locked the door. "You okay?" he asked.

Caro turned. Her lips were puffy and her cheeks still held a healthy glow from their encounter. "I'm fine. We need to go. It's a long way to Las Vegas." She headed for the door and Dell blocked her way.

"We aren't through, Caro."

"Yes, we are, Dell. We can't do this...you're a driver, and I own this team. It's not...we can't..."

He almost felt sorry for her, but if she'd felt half the passion he did, she had to know this wasn't something they could ignore. But he wouldn't push her to do something she wasn't ready to do. "Okay, Caro. We'll do this your way, for now. But we aren't through – far from it."

Chapter Seven

Caro reached for the door latch, and Dell let her go. She'd never... Never felt anything like the toe curling, bone-melting heat that ravaged her body. Never dreamed she could want...need anything as bad as she wanted and needed Dell Wayne. Thank God, Russell came looking for them, or no telling how far she would have let it go. Even now, her breasts craved his touch, and other places ached for what might have been.

Wrong. It was so wrong. She wasn't stupid. Rumors flew around the race circuit faster than a car without a restrictor plate. You couldn't be a woman in a man's world, especially one as driven by testosterone as this one, and not be subject to improper conjecture: but there was no reason to add reality to the fiction. She. Would. Not.

She scooted to the far side of the bench as Dell climbed into the electric cart beside her. She. Would. Not. Touch him. No matter how badly her fingers itched to feel all those hard muscles again. Oh, God. Why did it have to be Dell Wayne?

The chopper ride to the resort north of Phoenix took a lifetime, and when she met Dell later for dinner, she realized cold showers were totally overrated. One heated look from those blue eyes of his, and every want, every need came rushing back, only hotter and more urgent than before. She took the seat across the table from him, determined to put as much distance as possible between them.

"We can't do this," she said by way of greeting.

Dell lowered the menu in his hands and grinned. "Have dinner?" he asked.

"Don't be dense, Dell. You know what I'm talking about."

"We haven't done anything," Dell said, returning to his menu, "to my everlasting regret."

"Regret all you want, but making a success of this team is my primary goal right now, and I'm not going to blow it for a quickie in the hauler."

Dell lowered the menu again to look at her. The lazy grin was gone, replaced by a granite façade. "Two things, Caro." He paused until she met his gaze. "One: I don't see how our personal relationship has any bearing on whether Hawkins Racing succeeds or not. And two: what makes you think it was going to be a fast lap? I know when to go slow, and honey, we might have gotten off to a fast start, but there wasn't going to be anything quick about it, I assure you."

Caro clutched her menu as if it might sprout wings and fly at any second. Dell's assertion didn't do anything to shore up her resolve, but she wasn't going to tell him. She put on her best "business etiquette" face and said, "To address your issues...Number one: there are enough people waiting for me to fall on my face, or at the very least, steer Hawkins Racing into the wall without making the rumors of sexual favors a reality. If you don't think I know about the track talk, think again. I know what they're saying about me, and I know if the rumors became true, I'd lose even more ground. I've got plenty to prove, Dell – to myself, and to everyone who has ever said a woman can't own a successful race team.

"Number two: I've seen no evidence to indicate you've ever done anything slow." He opened his mouth to protest and Caro cut him off with a wave of her hand. He closed his mouth and she continued, using the opportunity to change the subject to the one they should be discussing anyway. "I don't know what's gotten into you, Dell Wayne, but you've got to rein in your impulses – on the track. You took too many chances today. Yeah, you won, but there were any number of stunts that could have ended badly for you and the car. You were lucky today – that's all. You didn't win because you were the best driver, or because you had the best car. You won because you were lucky."

"If you think that, you *don't* have any business running a race team. You may have something to prove, Caro, and I don't mind you using me to do it, but I drive to win, and as long as I'm the one in the car, I'll decide how best to go about it."

"Oh really?" Caro countered. "Well, that attitude lost you one ride this season already. It might cost you another."

"No, it won't. You aren't going to fire me, Caro. Who would drive for you? Wilson? You and I both know you aren't going to prove your point to anyone with him behind the wheel, so let's get this straight right now. I drive. I don't listen to non-drivers who think they can tell me how to do my job, and that includes you. I brought home a trophy for Hawkins Racing today. So, I didn't get another notch carved into my helmet after the race, but you got what you wanted – another notch carved in the stick you're trying to ram up everyone's butt. So how about this? I won't screw Hawkins Racing," his leer made his veiled meaning clear – "and you don't tell me how to drive? That way, we both get what we want."

Dell stood and tossed his menu on the table. "I'll see you at the airport," he said before stalking out of the restaurant leaving Caro stunned and alone.

She didn't know how long she sat, staring at the doorway, clutching the menu in a death grip, but when the waiter came to take her order, she dug some bills out of her purse and dropped them on the table. "I've changed my mind," she said. "I'm not hungry after all."

Dell was right about one thing. She wasn't going to fire him. She needed him. But that didn't give him license to drive like a maniac. Sure, she wanted him to win – that was the whole point of racing, of any competition, for that matter. But the way he was driving, she'd be lucky if he didn't drive Hawkins Racing right into bankruptcy. Today's purse would help, but the bottom line was, she couldn't afford for Dell to destroy many more cars, and still stay in business. The debts she inherited along with the race team were considerable.

As she gathered her things for the ride to the airport and their commuter flight to Las Vegas, she idly wondered if perhaps this had been her father's plan all along. He couldn't bear to sell the race team – it meant too much to him to do it while he was alive – but he hadn't wanted her to run it either. So maybe he left it in this sorry financial state in order to force her to sell. She did a quick estimate and decided if she sold right now, the assets – thanks to Dell's win today, would cover the debt with perhaps a little bit left over.

That was probably the smart thing to do, but it was also the one thing she wasn't going to do. She loved racing. Always had, and owning and running Hawkins Racing was her dream. Dell's win would keep her dream alive for another race or two, and if he won, or at least ran well in those, he would buy her more time. Somehow, she had to convince Dell to be more conservative on the track. The occasional win was nice, but consistently running in the top ten was good too.

They took the hotel shuttle to the airport in silence and cleared security before Caro decided it was time to address the other issue between them. Dell chose a seat in the waiting area facing the window with his back to the rest of the travelers. Caro ignored his cold shoulder as she joined him.

"Look, Dell. About what happened in the hauler…"

"It won't happen again," he said, without looking up from his magazine.

"We were both caught up in the moment, the win, and then the argument about how you won. From now on, let's not discuss the race until at least the next day. How's that? Give us some time to cool off – so to speak."

"Fine. Whatever you want. You're the boss."

Caro settled back in her seat and stared straight ahead. "Okay, I get it. You're still pissed you aren't going to get any, and you're placating me when you have no plans to discuss any race – ever."

"You're quick, I'll give you that," he said as he leisurely turned a page.

Caro sighed. This wasn't going to be easy. "Look, Dell. You and I both know I'm not going to fire you. But I do own the team, and I will give you my opinion about your driving. This is important to me – making a success out of the team. It's more than the thing about being a woman in a man's world. It's about proving to myself that my dreams are attainable. All my life, my dad told me I couldn't have my dream – not in so many words, you know, but in the things he did, like sending me away to school to keep me out of the garage. He said he wanted more for me than to marry some grease monkey, or heaven forbid, a driver. It never occurred to him I could be a team owner or that I might be good at building engines. All he ever saw for me was being someone's little woman, and he wanted that someone to be a doctor or a lawyer or anything, as long as he would keep me away from the track."

"Well, at least your dad believed what he was doing was in your best interest. I can't say the same for mine," Dell said.

"What do you mean?"

Dell shrugged. "Caudell was afraid…"

"Afraid of what? Afraid you'd kill yourself on the track? Because that's sure what it looks like you're trying to do."

Dell closed his magazine, using his index finger to hold his spot, and turned to her. "No, he was afraid I would be better than him, and he couldn't stand the thought of it. So you see, Caro. You and I are alike. We both have something to prove to our old men. So, you prove your point your way, and I'll prove my point my way."

And once again, Dell left her sitting all alone with thoughts spinning around in her head faster than a car going full throttle at Talladega.

～⁖～

Well, shit. Dell crammed his carry-on into the small overhead compartment. Caro Hawkins was going to be the death of him, despite her claim he was going to die on the track.

He settled into his seat, the one he'd requested in the back of the plane, as far away from hers as possible. Now that he'd touched her, tasted her, there was no turning back. His body yearned for hers like it never had for any other woman, but his brain – the big one – screamed for him to run as fast and as far away as possible. He pretended to read a magazine, but his mind was on Caro and his conflicting emotions where she was concerned. The physical reaction to her was simple enough – red-blooded male attracted to beautiful female. He didn't need to examine it too closely, but something about his reaction to her went beyond the usual. All he'd had was a sample, a tiny taste of Caro, and every cell in his body screamed for more. His gut clenched at the thought that maybe she was the one, the one he would never get enough of.

If that weren't enough to make a man run for the hills, nothing was. Dell glanced up the aisle and caught a glimpse of her sleeve peeking out from her seat in the front of the plane. Putting twenty rows of seats between them didn't constitute running, did it? No, running would be quitting the team. He could sit out the season. Hell, if he never raced again he'd live and eat well for the rest of his life on his old man's money. Dell turned his attention back to his long-forgotten magazine. Reality check. He wasn't going to give up racing. Like Caro, he had something to prove.

Which brought him to their airport conversation. What possessed him to tell her all that? He'd never told anyone about his strained relationship with his father. It wasn't much of a secret within the racing world, but most people were reluctant to mar the sterling reputation of his revered father. Fans still bought stuff with Caudell's name, number and likeness on it, as if his ghost were going to appear suddenly and win the fucking championship. No, they didn't want to hear about the real Caudell Wayne, Senior, the one Dell knew up close and personal. They'd never believe a man could say the things to his son Caudell had.

And to think how close he'd come close to telling Caro everything. Well, it wasn't going to happen. So, where did that leave them?

Sitting twenty rows apart on a plane with only twenty-three rows, and he didn't know about her, but it wasn't nearly enough distance to keep him from wanting her.

❧

"I want the car I drove last week," he said. "I know you think this one is something special, but Caro, trust me, it won't win here. Maybe on a short track, but not here."

"I designed this car myself, Dell. I know what it can do," Caro argued. "I made some adjustments, so get your ass in the car and take it out again."

Dell stared her down, but she refused to cower. She believed this car was the right one for this track and convincing her otherwise wasn't going to be easy.

"Unless you found a way to coax more RPM out of the engine, it's a waste of time, Caro. I'll take it out again, but it won't change the facts."

"That's all I'm asking, Dell. Take it out one more time. If the engine isn't performing up to standards, we'll use the backup car again."

"Whose standards are we talking about? Yours or mine?" he asked.

"Mine are the only ones that count," she said, holding her ground. Dell felt, rather than heard, the snickers coming from the crew. Caro could cut a man off at the knees when she wanted to.

Dell climbed into the car, pausing with his ass balanced on the door. "Get the backup car out of the hauler, guys. I'll be back in a minute." He dropped into the seat and buckled up. One more practice run to get Caro off his back, then he'd take the backup for a spin and show her what was what.

He had to give her credit. This car would be good on a short track where short bursts of speed were called for, but on a track like Vegas, or Phoenix, it couldn't sustain the level of power it needed to be competitive, much less win.

"Are you seeing what I'm seeing?" he spoke into his headset.

After a long pause, Caro came on. "Yes, I see. Damnit, Dell. That engine should be capable of more. I don't know what's wrong."

"I'm sure you'll figure it out, Caro. Now, can I have the backup car?" he asked.

"Take her to the hauler, Dell. We've already got the backup unloaded."

"Roger that. Comin' in," he said.

He switched cars, made a few practice runs with the car he won with in Phoenix, and after making a few suggestions to the crew, he went in search of Caro. He knew he should stay away from her, but goddamned, that fire suit of hers turned him on. All he had to do was look at her in the damned thing, and his body ignited. Add her air of confidence, her I'm-in-charge-so-do-as-I-say attitude, and he was ready to go five hundred laps with her.

He found her in the lounge at the front of the hauler, but she wasn't alone. She'd taken off the fire suit and replaced it with jeans and a Hawkins Racing V-necked T-shirt that hugged her curves like a driver's dream car. She was bent over an open book on the laminated desk that took up two walls of the lounge, pointing out something to the engineers flanking her. Dell's libido shot into overdrive, and he had no doubt the other two men in the room suffered from the same condition.

An unfamiliar emotion mixed and mingled with his raging hormones, and he fought to keep it in check. No matter how much Caro wanted to make her mark in the racing world and be recognized for her abilities, there was no way to avoid being recognized in other ways too. She was all woman – and there wasn't a man on the circuit who wouldn't notice. For the first time, he realized how big a task she'd set for herself.

He stifled his urge to grab her and drag her someplace where they could be alone – someplace he could show her how satisfying it was to be a woman, but she seemed oblivious to the way she affected the men around her, and she probably wouldn't appreciate him going caveman on her.

Instead of acting on his urges, he asked, "Figure it out yet?"

Caro straightened, and in the unguarded moment when she turned to him, he caught a glimpse of something that resembled desire in her eyes. But as quickly as it appeared, it vanished, and Caro, the team owner, spoke. "No, not yet. I have some ideas though. I was going over them with Frank and Terry. I don't know though, this engine may never be anything but a short track engine."

"Would that be a such a bad thing? We need a new short track car anyway," he said.

"Thanks to you, we do."

So, she hadn't forgotten about the wreck at Martinsville, or forgiven him for it. Dell shrugged. "Shit happens."

"Let's not go around the same old track again, Dell," she said, turning to her engineers. "Unless you guys have any other ideas, why don't you go make the new adjustment? After the official practice runs are over, we can take her back out for another run."

Dell moved away from the door as the other men filed out of the lounge, leaving him alone with Caro. Memories of them alone together the day before swamped him. That's all it had been, one day? Jesus, it seemed like forever since he'd touched her. He glanced her way and saw recognition in her eyes. She could deny it 'til the cows came home, but her eyes didn't lie. Desire burned in her gaze. He closed the distance between them, forcing her to look up at him.

"Caro," he said.

"Dell." She didn't move away, but she didn't move any closer either.

"Are you going to stop me?" he asked. His heart lodged in his throat as he waited for her answer. If she didn't want him to touch her, he wouldn't, but damn, he didn't understand how she could deny what was so obviously between them.

"We shouldn't," she said on a whisper.

"Who's to know, Caro?" He traced her jaw with his index finger and she trembled from just that tiny contact.

"We would," she said, but she still made no move away from his touch. He slipped his hand to her neck, letting his fingers curve around to her nape, and still, she didn't move away.

He dipped his head so his lips hovered over hers. "I won't tell." Then he kissed her. Her lips were soft under his, warm and damp from where her tongue touched them a breath ago. He brought his other hand up to cradle her face as he drank her in. God, she tasted sweet. He needed more.

Chapter Eight

She needed more. Even as she inwardly called herself all manner of names, she craved more. His thumbs pressed against her jaw, urging her to open for him. She groaned, pressed herself against him and let him in. He thrust his tongue past her lips and plundered. Her head spun as he took her on a wild ride that left her body achingly unsatisfied.

Caro silently begged for more, wrapping her arms around his neck and answering his kiss with all the passion coiled inside her. When his hand drifted to her waist, a desperation she'd never experienced took hold of her. She covered his hand with hers and guided his fingers beneath the waistband of her jeans. Their fingers tangled. His hand followed the zipper as it slid down and down, until he found her aching nub.

Her heart slammed against her ribcage and liquid heat pooled between her legs. She broke the kiss, gasping for breath. Still cradling the back of her head, Dell pressed her cheek against his chest and continued to explore between her legs. A single warning thought flashed, and like dry tinder, was devoured by the fire in her belly.

Dell's fingers dipped lower and she shifted to give him the room he needed. One finger slipped inside her, followed by another. The flames licked higher, threatening to consume her. A sound, a whimper, escaped her lips. Strong fingers stroked her head, soothing, calming. His words rumbled like a distant storm beneath the layers of his fire suit.

"Shh, sweetheart. Let go, Caro. I've got you."

He was dangerous, on and off the track. He drove like a demon with little regard to his or anyone else's safety, but in his arms, she was safe. Dell would always keep her safe.

Her legs became quivering, useless columns of gel, her only support the strong hand between her legs. Caro concentrated on the two pillars of steel impaling her, stroking some invisible spot that made her weak and energized her at the same time. Passion coiled tightly. Dell's voice vibrated against her cheek, her breasts, "Let go, sweetheart. I've got you."

The tight spring within gave way, and she came apart in his arms. Inner muscles clenched around his fingers and her vocal chords failed to form coherent sounds. Her body was a mess of discordant muscles and useless bones. She clung to him, her arms still draped over his shoulders. Time stood still. He slipped his fingers from her body, his hand from her jeans, and with a tenderness that brought tears to her eyes, he backed her to a chair and urged her to sit. Her arms fell to her sides and she reached for him, but he backed away.

He was at the door before she found her voice.

"You're leaving?" she asked.

"Yeah, I am," he said. "Before we turn rumor into fact."

Caro shivered as the blast of warm dry air from outside mingled with the cooler air inside against her bare skin. She jumped up, wobbling on shaky legs and zipped her jeans. "Damn you, Dell Wayne," she murmured to the closed door. "Damn you all to hell."

Dell fired the engine and listened to the familiar rumble. The caged power vibrated through him as he checked the gauges and waited for the race to begin. The thrill of competition sped through his system. He gripped the steering wheel with his left hand, the gearshift with his right, and tried to focus on the job at hand. He'd never been as distracted before a race as he was today. He'd never lain awake all night, remembering the feel of Caro Hawkins in his arms, or the taste of her lips, or the way her hot, wet heat clamped his fingers, or her face when she came. And the throaty whimper that accompanied her release.

Thankfully, he came to his senses before he let it go any further. It would have been so easy to take her. She wouldn't have said no, not the way she responded to him. But like she said, they had a business arrangement, and sex didn't figure into it.

He had to admire her. She was taking on a business that defined sexist. Sure, there were a few women in the business – a couple of drivers, some techs, and at least one mechanic he knew of. But the only female team owner was the wife of a driver, and she was only a partner in the business. No doubt, her husband's status helped her, where Caro was on her own. It took guts to do what she was doing.

But, damn, the woman was addictive. After their first kiss, he'd sworn he wouldn't touch her again. His resolve disappeared faster than rain in the desert, leaving him with an unquenchable thirst for Caro. The road she'd chosen was treacherous enough without him adding truth to the rumors flying around the circuit.

"We're good to go," Russell informed him.

"Everything looks good here," Dell said. "Let's race." He pushed thoughts of Caro out of his head. His foot tapped the throttle. He couldn't think of a better place to work out his sexual frustrations than on the racetrack, pitting man and machine against each other for five hundred grueling miles. If he were lucky, he'd be too tired tonight to think about Caro, to dream of driving more than just her car.

⤳⤳

Dell pushed harder, squeezing every drop of power out of the car. Fifty laps to go and his car was held together by crash tape and a prayer. He threaded his way between two slower cars on the backstretch, dropped low on turn three and traded paint with another car to climb one step closer to the front of the pack. He cursed the cluster of cars in front of him and kissed the bumper of the one directly ahead.

"Move over, asshole," he said.

"He's got nowhere to go, Dell," Jeff said into his headset.

"Then they've all got to go," he said, referring to the cars three wide out of turn four, blocking his way.

"Hang back. They'll break up on turn one," Jeff said.

A string of curse words flitted through Dell's mind, but he kept them to himself.

"Go high in one, drop low in turn two and you should be able to sweep underneath the 15 car," Jeff advised.

Dell tried the strategy, edging underneath the 15 car, but the driver wasn't ready to give up his track position. Dell jerked the steering wheel to the right, sideswiping the 15. The other driver

62

backed off immediately and Dell shot past him, one more position closer to the front of the pack.

Two cars ahead of him ran side-by-side through the backstretch. Dell waited while they jockeyed for position through turns three and four. As the car on the outside tried to regain his position, Dell throttled up and squeezed in between the two cars.

"Three wide," Jeff said, as if it were news to Dell.

Dell nudged the nose of his car ahead of the other two. Turn one loomed ahead. Neither of his adversaries was going to back down and let him go ahead. They couldn't go three wide through the turns. It was a high-speed game of chicken, and Dell wasn't going to be the first one to flinch. He throttled up when a prudent man would throttle back, but prudence was for stockbrokers, not stock car racers.

Adrenaline rushed through his system. This was the thrill he craved, the headlong plunge into unknown waters. The do or die scenario. The fight or flight reaction. The choice was easy for him. Do. Fight. What would the other drivers choose?

"Clear right," Jeff said.

Dell glanced in the rearview mirror and saw the car to his right drop back. He'd chickened out – chose flight. That left the car on his left. Dell matched his speed, hitting the throttle as much as he dared, edging ahead a little before his opponent matched him. They battled side-by-side for an entire lap.

Back to turn one, still side-by-side. Someone tapped him on the left rear panel and he instinctively tightened his grip on the wheel. He throttled up, hoping to push past the car now plastered bumper-to-bumper down the left side of his car as it propelled them both up the track. The wall sped closer. The muffled, but unmistakable sound of metal scraping on concrete penetrated his helmet, and in the same instant his car bounced off the wall and elementary physics came into play. *For every action there is an equal and opposite reaction.* And in Dell's opinion, the opposite reaction was rarely good.

Dell's car now became the one doing the pushing, maneuvering both cars back down the track toward the inside wall.

Screeching tires. Grinding, crumpling metal. The acrid stench of burning brake pads and disintegrating engines.

It took all of ten seconds, maybe less. Dell made a futile attempt to control his car as two, or was it three? others crashed into him, sending him careening one way, then another. The car tilted up on two wheels once, settled back, then spun a couple of dizzying three-hundred-sixty-degree turns before it mercifully came to a stop.

Smoke filled the interior, blinding him. Dell mentally took stock. Alive. Breathing. Hurting, but not seriously. Nothing broken. Car demolished.

"Dell?" Jeff's voice came through the headset.

"I'm okay. All clear?" Dell asked, waiting for an affirmation before he unhooked the restraint system and lowered the net on the driver's side window.

With his feet firmly on the ground, he removed his helmet, waved his hand over his head to indicate he was fine, and looked around. He counted half a dozen cars in varying stages of wreckage. Most wouldn't race again today, a few might make it back out for the last thirty laps. His wasn't one of them. But, damn, what a rush!

Only a true adrenaline junkie understood the thrill of a violent crash – one you could walk away from virtually unscathed.

❦

Caro counted to ten, then one hundred, then ten again. She would not go ballistic in front of her entire pit crew, and God-only-knew-how many other people, press included. By the time she finished counting, she was alone on top of the war wagon, and reasonably calm, given her state of mind. Dell was trying to kill her, and her business. It was the only explanation for what he'd done, and she wasn't just thinking about earlier in the week when he'd taken her to heaven, or at least awfully close, before leaving her without so much as a. "Thank you, ma'am."

She spent the rest of the week avoiding him as if he carried a deadly disease – which he did. She didn't know what the scientific name was, but it was commonly referred to as too damned sexy for his own good, on top of a serious case of arrogance. It was the latter that kept her away for the last six days and the former that kept her body yearning to be exposed to him again. And again.

Caro desperately wanted to get close to Dell, and sex had nothing to do with the reason why.

She climbed down from the war wagon and smiled for the reporter waiting to ask her about the race. The delay coming down gave her a few precious minutes to find a smile to put on her face, and think of something to say besides the truth. The racing world was full of sharks, and the pool they all swam in was relatively small. Even a hint of weakness, and the others would sense blood in the water. Then it was all over. No caution flag to give you a chance to get your shit together. No restart on equal footing. The predator sharks would pick your crew off one at a time, and your creditors would show up on your doorstep, padlocks in hand.

Caro smiled at the reporter, who smiled at the camera lens before she launched into the interview – leaving Caro no choice but to participate. Anything else would be interpreted as just what it was – weakness.

"I'm here with Carolina Hawkins," she said into the microphone, "owner of Hawkins Racing." She turned to Caro. "Ms. Hawkins, what can you tell us about the wreck? Is Dell okay?"

"I haven't heard the official word, but Dell indicated he was fine, just a little bunged up, which is to be expected. AARA does an excellent job of making sure the cars are safe."

"Given what happened to Caudell Senior, Dell's father, I'm sure this kind of thing must be especially difficult for Dell. How does he handle it?"

Caro resisted the urge to laugh. Was she kidding? Dell drove like every race was a demolition derby – that's how he handled it. A sudden thought chilled her blood. Could it be deliberate? No. She'd mentioned it to him before. No. It wasn't possible. Stupid to think that.

She pushed the thought away and gave the expected answer. "As you know, there have been many improvements in the safety systems within the cars since Caudell Wayne's accident. Dell knows better than most how dangerous stock car racing is. He takes every precaution, and follows every safety guideline – just as we all do at Hawkins Racing."

"Do you know what caused today's crash?" she asked.

Arrogance. Stupidity. Suicidal tendencies? "Which one?" she asked instead of voicing her actual thoughts.

The reporter laughed. "I guess that was a stupid question," she said. She turned away to address the reporters in the booth, dismissing Caro.

She couldn't get out fast enough.

She found Russell, told him she was leaving, and headed for the chopper pad. She needed to talk to Dell, but not until she took some time to consider what she would say. If what she was thinking were true, Hawkins Racing was in trouble, and Dell was in even worse trouble.

༄༅྾

Her head spun with the possibility that instead of hiring a driver who would help her save Hawkins Racing from bankruptcy, she'd hired one whose death wish would murder her company in the process. No matter how she looked at the bottom line, it didn't get any better. Debt and bad luck were sucking Hawkins dry faster than a vampire horde in a blood bank. If things didn't turn around soon, she'd be penning the bottom line in her own blood, unable to afford the red ink.

Caro closed her eyes and willed the ugly truth to go away. One more crash like the one in Las Vegas, and Hawkins Racing was done for. She'd have to dip into the reserve fund – the tiny bank account on the side – to pay for the parts to build a new car. Thanks to Dell's recklessness, they were down to one – and in his own words, it wasn't a winner.

She allowed herself a few minutes to absorb the grim reality of her situation. What seemed like a good idea a few weeks ago, now smacked of the worst decision of her life. If she'd kept Jeff... well... not a thing would have changed. Sure, she wouldn't be wondering how to pay for the parts they needed – but she'd still be wondering how long the company could hang on. Jeff wasn't ready to race at this level, perhaps he never would be. He wouldn't have won any races, but he didn't crash either. At least, she'd still have a car to put on the track.

Then there was Dell, or more specifically, *Dell*. Being the pragmatic woman she was, she had to admit one of the reasons she'd gone to him in the first place – besides the fact he was about the only Cup driver without a ride in the middle of the season – was that she'd had a crush on him since she was a kid. One of the worst things about being sent away to school – worse than leaving her dad and the circuit behind – was leaving Dell. She wasn't idiot enough to believe he'd harbored any feelings for her. Not a man like Dell. He was everything a track bunny dreamed of, and lord, help them all when he put on a fire suit.

Caro still remembered the first time she'd seen him in one. He was all of sixteen and full of excitement before his first Nationwide Series race. He won the race, and several more that year. She remembered the way the reporters talked about him. He was a phenomenon. He was bringing a new, smarter style of racing to the sport. They held him up as the driver of the future – one who would change racing from the "revenuers-on-my-ass" style, to a thinking man's sport.

But Dell had changed, and Caro had allowed her hormones to have a voice in her business decisions. It was a rookie mistake, and one she had to correct – somehow. The more time she spent with him, the more troublesome those hormones became. All Dell had to do was look at her and she wanted more. Good heavens, she wanted more. More of the heat he stirred within her, more of his touch, more, more, more.

The heavy outside door clanged shut, jolting Caro out of her erotic musings. She needed to keep, or more precisely, get her relationship with Dell back on a professional level. He was her employee, and it was her responsibility to set the tone for their association. No more touching him, and most importantly, no more letting him touch her.

Footsteps and voices in the hallway announced the arrival of her crew. It was another race week, and there was work to do. Another car to build, parts to order and payroll to make. And, she still needed to talk to Dell – preferably before he put his butt in another one of her cars and tried to kill himself. As his employer, she had a responsibility to keep him alive – didn't she? At the very least, it was in her best interest.

It was his day off and she debated whether to have the conversation with him or wait. As far as she could tell, Dell's suicide of choice was by automobile – on a racetrack – so perhaps the conversation could keep for at least one more day. And that would be one more day to convince herself to ignore her hormones. Besides, if Dell wanted to kill himself, he didn't need a racecar to do it. It was an unsettling thought, but one she quickly dismissed because deep down, she couldn't believe suicide was Dell's motive. That begged the question, "What was?"

If he weren't trying to kill himself on the track, there had to be something else behind his reckless driving style.

"Got a minute?" Russell leaned in her open doorway. The deep furrow between his eyebrows told Caro this wasn't a social call.

"Sure," she said. "You know I always have time for my crew chief." Russell shuffled in, shutting the door behind him. Even though she was the one in the power position behind the desk, Caro's stomach flipped. It was going to take more than a few months to get used to being the one in charge. "Have a seat," she said.

Russell took the chair across from her, sat forward, his elbows resting on his knees. He let out a puff of air through pursed lips, as if reconciling himself to an unpleasant duty. Dread wrapped itself around Caro's somersaulting stomach and squeezed.

"What is it, Russell?"

"I dunno know how to say this, Carolina, so I'm gonna to come right out with it."

Russell paused. Caro's shoulders tightened, and she mentally chided herself for being ridiculous. What could Russell possibly say that could be worse than her own thoughts these days? Her black thoughts of a minute ago flashed through her head, and the band of dread gripping her stomach wrapped itself around her heart. "Is this about Dell?"

"No...well..." he stammered.

"Is he alright?"

Russell's gaze snapped to hers. "Why wouldn't he be?"

The bands around her insides loosened and her shoulders relaxed a fraction. "No reason," she waved away her concerns. "Go on."

"I thought you should know... people are talkin'...sayin' things..."

"Such as?"

Every moment he hesitated, Caro imagined another possible horrific scenario. "Just spit it out, Russell. Whatever it is."

"Some of the guys went out for a drink after the race. They heard some people talkin' about you. And Dell."

Caro clenched her fists in her lap. Seriously? Was she going to have to get a pair of pliers and yank the story out of him? "What did they say?"

"That you and Dell...were, you know..."

"They think I'm sleeping with Dell."

"Yeah, that's the story goin' around." Russell sat up, squaring his shoulders. "You're both adults, and what you do ain't none of our business, unless it reflects on Hawkins Racing. As long as you're runnin' the team, people are gonna to talk. Your daddy was right. This ain't any place for a woman."

His words stung, and Caro sat for a moment, unable to take it all in. She matched Russell's firm posture and looked him in the eye. "You're right about one thing, Russell. My personal life isn't anyone's business. As for this not being my place, well, I don't care what

68

anyone thinks. I own Hawkins Racing, and I intend to run it." Russell squirmed under her counter-attack. Caro continued. "If you or anyone else in the garage doesn't want to work for a woman, then you're free to go. Good luck finding another place in the middle of the season."

Her take-no-prisoners attitude took some air out of Russell's tires. "No, no." He slapped his hands on his knees. "The crew ain't going anywhere. We all believe in Hawkins Racing." Caro would have smiled at how fast he shifted into reverse if she hadn't been so angry.

"Then why bring it up? What's this really about?"

"I think you should sell."

"To who?" she asked.

"I hear Renfro might make you a good offer. Your daddy was friends with Butch Renfro. He'd approve if you were to sell."

The band around her stomach tightened again. So, the old boys network was trying to force her out, and using her own crew to do it. "And how do you know this?" she asked.

"Well, he told me."

"He told you," Caro enunciated each word as she let the knowledge settle in. "When?"

"'Bout the time you took Dell on, I guess."

"So why did you wait until now, and more important, why didn't Butch come to me with the offer?"

Russell squirmed again. Caro sighed. His body language answered for him. "He told you to wait, didn't he? He told you to wait, to see how we did. What was it? Owner points? Driver points? Wins?"

"Owner points. Look, Carolina. Butch is only doin' what he knows your daddy wanted. This is no – "

"Place for a woman. Yeah, I've heard it before." Caro leaned back in her chair and tried to look calm while she seethed inside. "You can tell Butch Renfro Hawkins Racing isn't for sale, and I'm going to act like this conversation never took place." Instead of falling apart like she wanted to, Caro sucked up all her courage and issued orders. There'd be plenty of time to hit the wall later.

"We only have a few days to build a car for Darlington. Use the frame from the Bristol car and the short track engine we tested at Las Vegas. I have some changes I want to make to the engine and the trim. Get the crew started. I'll consult with the engineers about the changes while you get started on the teardown. Oh, and salvage what you can from the Las Vegas engine. We'll rebuild it and use it in Charlotte. We've got the All-Star week coming up. We'll need everything we've got to get through it."

As soon as Russell was out of her office, Caro crossed her arms on her desk and dropped her forehead on top. She took a couple of deep breaths and refused to give in to the panic threatening to take her under. Doubts crept in. Maybe she wasn't ready to run the business. Maybe her father had been right all along. Another deep breath. She sat up and looked around the office. Her office. Her business.

So, things weren't going as smoothly as she hoped. As far as she was concerned, the race was far from being over, and as long as she kept a car on the track, there was a chance of a decent finish, if not a win.

Pain throbbed behind her temples. Caro yanked the elastic band loose that was wrapped around her high ponytail. Her hair tumbled to her shoulders. She shook it out, smoothed it back and secured it at the neck. She found a couple of aspirin and washed them down with cold coffee.

She reminded herself she'd always been a "glass-half-full" kind of person. Dell gave her some excellent feedback regarding her new engine, and there were a few things she wanted to try. If they worked, this engine could be the one that would make Hawkins Racing a force to be reckoned with on the circuit, provided she could keep her driver alive, and her car in one piece. Caro sifted through the stacks on her desk, looking for her notebook.

She flipped through it until she found what she was looking for. She wasn't ready to give up on her dream yet. As long as the doors remained open, there was still hope of saving her family legacy, and creating one of her own.

Chapter Nine

Dell stood in the middle of the track, his hands fisted on his hips, his eyes masked by dark glasses. He made it a point to arrive a day earlier than everyone else to this particular track – a bi-annual, grim pilgrimage of sorts. Dubbed, "The Lady in Black" because Darlington was the first track to be paved with asphalt, the moniker seemed more fitting to Dell than the newer, "Too Tough to Tame" nickname. This track, more than any other, would always remind him of dark times. It was here he had his last, harsh argument with his father, and here, on the final turn, where his father's life came to an end.

He put one foot in front of the other until he stood on the exact spot where Caudell Wayne drew his last breath. Dell looked at his feet. Heat from the sun-baked asphalt radiated up through the soles of his shoes. The wall had been repainted dozens of times since the wreck, but still, Dell found it hard to look at. He took a deep breath and raised his eyes to the section of concrete in front of him, not for the first time wondering if Caudell sensed in the split-second before he hit that it was the end.

Dell didn't see the wreck. He'd been too far out in front on the final lap. He still remembered his spotter's voice congratulating him on the win, and in the next breath, telling him Caudell crashed.

"There's a crash behind you, turn four. Your dad's involved," he said.

"Anyone else?" Dell asked.

"No," he hesitated, "it doesn't look good, Dell."

By that time, Dell was around the track on his victory lap. "I see it." The last cars were dodging the wreck. A silence Dell couldn't explain filled his car. He heard nothing. No engine noise. No crowd yelling. Not even his spotter or crew chief. Caudell's car sat perpendicular to the wall, utterly still except for a cloud of steam curling up from the crushed radiator. Dell braked, coming to a stop with the nose of his car a few feet from the passenger side door of his father's car, giving him a clear view inside.

He knew before he unfastened his restraint system, before his feet hit the asphalt, before he rushed around to the driver's side. It was too late.

The Lady in Black, silent as the night, wrapped herself around him as he stared through the window net at his father's lifeless body and tried to find some emotion within him stronger than the anger coursing through his veins.

Dell raised his eyes to the sky, as flawlessly blue today as it had been dark that night. "Stupid, fucker. You never did listen to reason. It was your way, or the highway, and look where that got you." Silence answered him. He turned to go when the glint of sun on metal caught his eye. He bent down and picked up the nickel-plated washer. It was hot from the sun-heated asphalt. Dell pinched it between his thumb and forefinger. A sign? Yeah, he chuckled to himself – a sign someone else fucked up on this stretch of track. He palmed the coin-sized piece of metal and curled his hand into a fist.

He turned back to the wall, and with every ounce of strength he possessed, he chucked the washer at the wall. It hit with a metallic ping and ricocheted across the track, out of sight.

"Take that, you goddamned hard-headed son-of-a-bitch."

❦

"Can I see you for a minute?" Caro asked.

"Sure," Dell said, taking the seat next to her in the golf cart. "I've got a few minutes."

Caro set the cart in motion. Dell admired the lines of her legs and arms as she steered the cart. "Where're we going?"

"Someplace we can talk," she said.

The further she drove away from the relative civilization around the track, the more worried he became. When she'd passed the last row of motor homes in the fan parking area and kept on going, Dell realized nothing good could come of this conversation. He looked around at the empty field that would fill in the next few days, but for now, was nothing more than pastureland. "I'm beginning to think this may be a one-way ride for one of us," he said.

"No. I'll give you a ride back." She finally stopped the cart, but she didn't seem in any hurry to start the conversation she said she wanted.

"What's up, Carolina?"

"Look, Dell. I'm worried about you."

Dell chuckled. "Seriously? Why?"

"It's the way you drive – on the track, I mean. I have no idea how you drive off the track."

Her nervous babbling didn't help one bit. "Just tell me, Caro. What is it you had to drag me out to the middle of nowhere to say?"

"I know I've asked you before, but it was a rhetorical question then. This time, I'm serious, Dell. I really want to know. Are you trying to kill yourself? Is that why you drive the way you do?"

Dell focused on an arriving motor home in the distance, slowly making its way across the grass to one of the chalk-lined parking spaces. She couldn't know how wrong she was, and he wasn't going to tell her. "No."

"Then why, Dell? What goes through your head when you're racing? Because I can tell you, I'm not the only person who thinks you drive like a suicidal maniac."

The motor home made three attempts to back into a space where there wasn't a single neighbor. Dell watched in silence.

"Talk to me," Caro said. "I'm only trying to help, Dell."

"Are you firing me?" he asked. He couldn't lose another ride. Racing was the one thing that kept him sane.

"No! Good heavens, no, Dell. I'm trying to figure out... oh, hell. I don't know what I'm doing." He didn't dare look at her, but he heard her frustrated sigh and noticed the way her whole body slumped. "Damnit, Dell. You can't keep going the way you are. You're going to get killed. The other drivers hate you. More than a few would take you out at the first opportunity if it weren't for the way your dad died." She stopped, as if she'd said too much. Dell kept silent watch as the motor home driver attempted to level his rig. If Caro thought he was going to participate in this conversation, she was sadly mistaken.

"I'm sorry. That was inappropriate," she finally said. "I'm concerned, Dell. That's all."

He kept his mouth shut.

"Okay, I get it. You don't want to talk about it, and maybe bringing the subject up at this track wasn't a good idea, but I don't want you to get hurt."

"Are you worried about me, Caro, or worried about your car?"

"I won't lie to you. Both. I'm worried about both, because the only time I need to worry about either is when the two converge."

Yeah, right. No way was he going to tell Caro his darkest secret – that the only time he felt in control was behind the wheel. The fact she worried about him at all was unexpected, and…nice. For that reason alone, she deserved something from him.

"Fair enough," he said. "If it's any consolation, I don't go out there looking for ways to wreck your car, or to hurt myself."

"Okay. Okay," she said. "That's reassuring."

"This conversation is over. Take me back."

She placed her foot on the gas pedal, then removed it. Dell slid his foot over to accelerate for her and she kicked him in the shin.

"Ow!"

"You deserved that," she said. "You're good, Dell." She shook her head. "I almost bought your act."

"It's not an act."

"Sure it is. You said all the things I wanted to hear. But it's what you aren't saying that I should be listening to."

"You can't listen to something I didn't say."

"That's where you're wrong, Dell. I believe you when you say you aren't trying to hurt yourself while you're driving, but you were very specific about that. And you're off the track more than you're on it. So, Dell, are you suicidal off the track?"

Dell watched as another motor home made its way across the grass to a parking space. Why couldn't Caro mind her own business? "Look, Caro, I don't want to drag you into the fucked up world inside my head. I'm not going to kill myself. I promise you that."

"Well, that's good. But it still doesn't explain why they call you Madman."

Dell sighed and released the tension holding his back straight. Damn, why did this woman make him want to tell her everything? It felt good to know someone cared, but he was coping well enough. As long as he kept busy, the memories didn't bother him so much. "I'm aggressive on the track. Some people don't like it, that's all. I'm not trying to kill myself or anyone else, I assure you. It's sweet of you to care, but I'd appreciate it if you let me fight my own demons, Caro, in my own way."

"Okay," she said, pressing on the gas pedal, setting the cart in motion. "But you better not be lying to me, Dell Wayne, or I'll kill you myself."

෴

Dell dropped the net and scrambled out through the window. He'd had enough of Richard Warner to last him a lifetime.

He tossed his helmet into the car and looked around. Dick Warner's car was a mangled mess, but the son-of-a-bitch was still inside, trying to restart it.

"Not today," Dell vowed as he crossed the track to Warner's car. Cars sped by under the yellow caution flag, even as Dell threw caution to the wind. As he walked, he pulled off his gloves and let them fall to the pavement. He wanted to experience the feel of Warner's skin beneath his fingers as he choked the life out of him. After nearly four hundred laps of putting up with Warner's shit, Dell was through. Through pretending Warner was a good driver. Through pretending the bastard hadn't meant to shove Caudell Senior into the wall. Through pretending it didn't matter. And he was damn well through letting Warner try to do him the same favor.

Dell fisted his fingers in the safety net covering the driver's window, and yanked. The netting fell free and Warner turned toward him. His helmet covered most of his face so Dell only saw Warner's eyes. Eyes filled with disbelief and a white-hot rage that mirrored Dell's.

"Get out, Warner. We're going to settle this right here and now," Dell said through gritted teeth.

Warner gave up trying to restart his car. He drew his gloves off, then his helmet. "If that's the way you want it, C.J."

Dell's vision clouded with a red haze. He stepped back far enough for Warner to get one leg out. He grabbed Warner by the collar and dragged him the rest of the way.

"Don't you ever call me that," Dell said. Then he planted his fist in Richard Warner's face.

Warner responded with a punch of his own. Dell dodged it, connected a left jab to Warner's mid-section and another right to his jaw. Warner stumbled backwards, but before Dell came at him again, he lunged forward.

Dell absorbed the blow to his chin and retaliated with another series of punches that connected with satisfactory auditory stimuli.

"What the fuck?" Warner yelled over the roar of engines buzzing past.

"You fucking killed Caudell, and I'll be damned if I'm going to let you kill me too," Dell answered between jabs to Warner's abs and jaw.

"It was an accident, you asshole," Warner countered.

"Accident my ass," Dell said as he landed another punch.

"What's it to you, bro? You got everything the old man had," Warner said as he buried his right fist in Dell's stomach. Dell doubled over, gasping for breath. Someone grabbed his arm and pulled him backwards. Another set of hands wrapped around his other arm and before he found his footing, he was in the back of an ambulance.

"Let me go," he growled as he lunged for the door.

"You aren't going anywhere but to the track medical center," the medic said. He knocked on the roof, and the ambulance lurched into motion.

Dell refused treatment. All his injuries were from Dick Warner's knuckles, and those would be gone soon enough. As he made his way to his motor home, Warner's final words echoed in his mind. What did he mean by them? Of course Dell got everything. He was an only child. Why wouldn't he? Did Warner think that was reason enough for Dell to want his father dead?

Hell, he couldn't care less about the money. He'd already given a huge chunk of it away, and he'd give the rest away as soon as he figured out the best way to do it. If he suddenly started living like a pauper, people would notice and wonder. He'd have to let them think he blew the money or tell them the truth. And the truth was none of their business.

‹‹›

Too Tough to Tame. That's what they said about Darlington. The same could be said about Dell Wayne, though "Too Wild to Tame" might be more accurate. Her little talk with Dell accomplished nothing.

He was still alive, but she had another wrecked car. Another Did Not Finish to post, and on top of that – a fine to pay. Dell's fistfight with Richard Warner, in the middle of the track – while cars dodged the wreckage – resulted in a fine for Hawkins Racing and a personal fine for Dell.

Caro tried to think positive thoughts. Having refused a ride through the tunnel to her motor home, she welcomed the painful jolt of each hard step on the concrete walkway. It gave her something to think about, something to be angry at besides Dell. She needed to get out of there, as far away from him as possible or she might be facing criminal charges along with another fine. In her present state of mind, Dell and Warner's altercation might look like a brawl on a kindergarten playground compared to what she wanted to do to Dell Wayne.

What the hell had he been thinking? AARA drivers don't fight each other. And they especially don't fight in the friggin' middle of a race! Stupid. And juvenile. And even more stupid. Stupider than stupid.

How he got off with a fine and no suspension was beyond comprehension. If she came up with the money to pay her share of the fine, Dell would race next week – provided she managed to put a car together. Caro snorted. The last thing she thought she would be doing was mentally calculating the price of scrap metal, hoping it would amount to enough to keep the doors open another week.

It was a short drive home, by AARA standards, but long enough to give Caro time to calm down and reassess her situation. Maybe selling scrap metal to pay the bills was a bit of an exaggeration, but not by much. Hawkins Racing couldn't take many more hits like the one today. Not only had they lost another car and been fined, but Dell's fistfight would bring unwanted talk. Speculation was running rampant already, fueled by the reporters who delighted in scandal. Caro sighed. She still needed to talk to Dell's sponsor, convince them to continue their support, or the scrap metal idea might come to fruition after all. How could she justify Dell's behavior? She'd seen the footage of the altercation. Dell was the one who started it, confronting Warner so the man had no choice but to defend himself. Though it did appear Warner threw a few punches that weren't strictly in self-defense.

Whatever.

There wasn't any excuse for two grown men punching on each other.

ะงจ๑

The last person Dell expected to see on his doorstep was Richard Warner.

"Can I come in?" Richard asked.

Curiosity got the best of him, and Dell stood back, indicating Richard should enter. Since their brawl on the track the night before, Warner's words continued to echo through Dell's mind, taunting him with the certainty that there was something behind them – something he should know.

"It's Mother's Day, don't you have some place to be?" he asked as he closed the door. He walked past Warner, expecting the man had enough sense to follow him, though he wasn't at all sure it was the case.

"No. I haven't seen my mother in three years."

"Funny, I took you for a momma's boy," Dell said, grabbing a beer from the refrigerator. He held up the bottle. "Want one?"

"No. I'm driving."

"Well, aren't you the Boy Scout." Dell pulled a diet soda out of the refrigerator and tossed it at his guest. Warner caught it with one hand and murmured his thanks. Dell leaned against the counter and took a long pull from the bottle. As far as he was concerned, he'd offered enough hospitality.

"Look, Dell... I think we need to talk."

What was it with everyone these days wanting to talk. First Caro, now Dickhead Warner.

"You think?" Dell pushed away from the counter and headed to the family room where he dropped into his favorite recliner. "You killed Caudell, and now you're trying to kill me. What's to talk about?"

Warner perched on the edge of the sofa, rolling the unopened soda can between his palms. "It was an accident, Dell. I didn't mean to kill him. I only wanted to get past him. I needed the track position points."

"Well, that makes me feel better. My old man is dead because you needed four points." Dell stood. "I appreciate you coming by to explain that to me, Warner." Dell pointed toward the front door. "I trust even an idiot like you can find your own way out."

"Sit down, Dell. I'm not through," Warner said.

Dell stared at him for a tense second before deciding throwing Warner out would be too much trouble. He sat. "Say what you came to say, then get out of my house."

"I'm here to apologize. You can't seriously believe I wanted to kill my own father."

"Whoa!" Dell sat up. "What the hell are you talking about?"

Warner went still, then he set the soda on the coffee table with exaggerated care. Finally, he looked at Dell. "Caudell was my father, too."

Dell shot out of his seat as if Warner lit a firecracker under him. "What the fuck? Are you out of your mind?" A red haze clouded his vision.

Warner stood. "I thought you knew, Dell. Honestly, I did or I wouldn't have come here." He shifted on his feet. "Look, can we sit down and talk about this?"

Dell paced to the doorway and back again before he sat. Warner followed his lead and perched on the edge of the sofa.

"I don't know what you think you're doing, Warner, but it isn't going to work. I think I'd know if I had a brother." It had to be some kind of sick joke, though a little voice deep inside warned him it might be true. He refused to acknowledge the sinister thought.

"Well, welcome to my world, Dell. I didn't know I had a brother either, or a father for that matter, until the day Caudell died. I felt bad enough about the way it happened, then Butch came up and clapped me on the back. He said something about how Caudell would have seen the irony of the situation. I stood there, staring at him. I think he realized I didn't know what he was talking about. He told me Caudell was my father. I don't know what I did afterwards. It's mostly a blur."

"He lied," Dell said, positive now this had to be a hoax. He just couldn't figure out who had anything to gain by it. Renfro? Warner? Maybe.

"I didn't believe him either. I never met my dad. Didn't know who he was. All my mother ever told me was that he was the love of her life, but they couldn't be together. I never understood why. Kids don't ask about stuff like that, you know? Anyway, the next day was Mother's Day. My mom was there for the race. You know, everyone's mother is honored before the race."

"I wouldn't know about that," Dell said.

"No, I guess you wouldn't," Warner said. "Sorry."

"I'm not asking for your pity," Dell said.

"And you won't get it," he said before he continued. "Anyway, it took a while for me to get to her." He paused. "I had to answer a lot of questions from the AARA officials. And there was a shit-load of reporters. I still don't know what I told them. I guess I said something, because they left me alone after that. I finally tracked down Mom at her hotel. I didn't even have to ask. She was a mess, crying, yelling. You don't need to know all of it; just that she blamed me for killing the only man she ever loved – and I guess that included me, because she said she never wanted to see me again. I haven't seen her since."

Silence descended on the room. Dell forgot all about his unfinished beer. Memories of all the times Caudell compared him to Warner, and found Dell wanting. Even on the day he died – apparently at the hands of his beloved, bastard son – he'd scolded Dell for not being more like Warner. His gut churned as a white-hot anger began to burn inside him. Snippets of conversation, moments frozen in time and seared on his mind. They made sense in light of Warner's declaration, and the flame of hate burned brighter. Warner continued as if he hadn't just opened the gates of hell and let all the demons run loose.

"So look, Dell. I admit I've been out to get you – not kill you. You're my brother, and probably the only family I've got. For a long time, I resented you. You had everything I didn't. You had our dad all to yourself, and I never had him at all. I went through a period where I hated you for getting all the money he left."

Dell jerked his gaze from the stubborn spot on the carpet to Warner. His brother held up a staying hand. "I'm over it now. It was petty, I know, but it's taken me a while to assimilate all this. I don't care about the money. I just want to understand why Caudell never made me a part of his life."

Dell chuckled. Oh, if Warner only knew how Caudell had felt about him. But he'd be damned if he was going to share the information with him. That was a private pain, and if Warner suffered for it, so much the better.

.

Chapter Ten

"Are you through?" Dell asked through gritted teeth.

"Almost. I'll admit to jealousy and to trying to make your life miserable, placing blame where it didn't belong, but I'm not trying to kill you." Warner stood and took a few steps toward the door before he stopped and turned to Dell. "I'm not expecting us to become a family, and I'm not going to tell anyone else about this, us, I mean. I figure if Butch knows, other people know. I'm tired of the all the fighting on the track – in the cars and out. From now on, if I go after you on the track, it's about track position and nothing else."

Dell sat corpse still, absorbing everything Warner said long after his bastard brother was gone. As bizarre as it was, it cleared up a lot of things Dell never understood growing up. His mother went away when he was five years old, leaving Dell with his father. One day she was there, and the next she was gone. He remembered crying buckets for months after she left, but the only explanation Caudell ever gave him for her defection was when Dell was about ten. Dell said something about how he wished he had a mother, and Caudell's response still stunned him. His father looked him in the eye and said, "She didn't understand men. We have needs."

Yeah, needs. Caudell always had someone to take care of his *needs*. His father's indiscriminate affairs disgusted Dell. Caudell never tried to hide the track bunnies he brought back to their motor home, but none of them ever stayed more than one night, or a few hours. No doubt, Warner's mother had been one of them.

Dell shook his head. It was a wonder there weren't a dozen more bastard siblings out there. Who knew? If there was one, there could be more.

But did he believe Warner? He mulled it over and came to the conclusion that yes, he did. Did his revelation change anything? It remained to be seen. Just because they shared the old man's blood didn't mean Dell was going to cut Warner any slack during a race. Dell raced to win, no matter who was on the track. If Warner wanted to back off from his vengeance against Dell, that was his prerogative. But it didn't mean Dell had to do the same. He didn't give a good goddamned about familial blood, especially if it stood between a checkered flag and him.

❧

Caro stood at the back of the crowd gathered outside the Charlotte Speedway, watching Dell sign autographs for his fans. He looked both hot and *hot* in his fire suit. Caro fanned herself with the folder in her hand. The hot wind she stirred up did nothing to cool her sun-baked skin or the warmth melting her from the inside out. Damn. Why did the sight of Dell do these things to her? He infuriated her at every turn –professionally and personally. And there wasn't a thing she could do about either one.

She might need him professionally, but on a personal level, he was the last thing she needed, and everything she wanted. It was a sad truth she'd come to accept. Popular psychology said recognizing a problem was the first step to overcoming it, so she'd taken the first step, admitting to herself how badly she wanted Dell Wayne. So far, admitting her weakness hadn't done a thing toward making it go away. If anything, the dreams that woke her at night became worse since her self-revelation.

And the worst of it was, she knew how his hands felt on her skin, how his lips felt on hers. It was knowledge she wished she didn't have because you couldn't unlearn something like that. It was as if his hands imprinted themselves on her skin, and like a tattoo, the imprint was etched in permanent ink. Caro chuckled to herself, imagining tattoos covering her body, announcing every few inches, "Dell was here."

Dell smiled at a teenage fan, and Caro shifted her gaze to the show car behind him rather than see his eyes sparkle at the girl. She'd seen enough women of all ages simper when he turned his megawatt smile on them to last her a lifetime.

The weatherman promised a solid week of record temperatures – exactly what they needed for the ten-day racing extravaganza that ended with the six-hundred-mile race on the following Sunday. Thankfully, it was close to home. Hawkins Racing didn't need two weeks of travel expenses on top of everything else. If Dell didn't finish well in either the All Star Shoot-Out or the Sprint Cup, they'd be taking the show car off the promo circuit for real. It was old as the hills, but with a minimum rebuild, it could meet today's safety standards and comply with the rule changes since it was taken out of commission.

Caro glanced at her watch, then at the crowd still seeking Dell's autograph. She weighed her desire to get out of the sun with the promise of souvenir sales if these women left here happy and decided a few more minutes in the heat wouldn't kill either of them. Dell glanced her way, his eyebrow raised in question. She flashed him five fingers. A slight twitch of his lips told her he wasn't happy about the time extension. But he didn't know how strapped they were for cash. These last two weeks of May at Charlotte had the potential to boost a team's bottom line if the drivers played nice with the fans. Thus, Caro booked Dell at every fan event possible. He was even sacking groceries at the tented grocery store in the middle of the campground one evening this week.

It was a grueling schedule of practice runs, qualifying, racing and promotion that would take a toll on anyone, even an athlete in top physical condition. It would also mean no time for fooling around with track bunnies or...her. By the time Dell was through every night this week, he wouldn't want to do anything but sleep. She only hoped she would be as lucky.

Four-and-a-half minutes later, Caro skirted the crowd and slipped in beside Dell. The women still wanting an autograph or photo voiced their displeasure. Caro handed out flyers detailing Dell's multiple appearances, assuring them they had ample opportunities still to get what they wanted. Dell signed one more hat before Caro shoved him in the direction of the track gate. He didn't need much encouragement. Caro hustled to keep pace with him. He slowed once he was in the hot-pass zone – away from all but the most privileged fans.

Caro followed blindly. Between the heat and her semi-run to the infield, she was past caring where they were going. Dell held the motor coach door open for her, his hand on the small of her back, and propelled her up the steps and inside. Cool air slammed against her, taking her breath away. Dell's body pressed against her backside, his hands came to rest on her hips. Her internal temperature spiked and her head whirled. Dell caught her as she began to fall.

"Sit down." He half walked, half carried her to the sofa, before he spun her around and used his hands to press her hips into a sitting position. "Loosen your blouse. I'll get you some water."

Caro fumbled with the buttons of her silk blouse. The fabric fell open down the front. Goosebumps rose on her exposed flesh as the cool air hit her.

❧

Damn. He didn't want to care about Carolina, but someone sure as hell needed to. It was obvious she wasn't taking care of herself. Dell wet a towel and grabbed two water bottles from the refrigerator. Since Warner's revelation, Dell thought of little else. Memories and reality collided until the pieces of the puzzle began to slip into place, and the picture they formed was ugly – filled with anger and hate that gnawed away at him.

He'd only found relief in his dreams, dreams of Caro, beneath him, riding him, taking him away from reality, taking him to paradise and beyond.

He stopped dead when he saw her.

She'd undone her blouse, revealing perfect breasts encased in some sort of lace marvel that married engineering with sin, and sent blood rushing to his cock with enough speed to make him dizzy. Caro's head rested on the back of the sofa, her eyes closed, her full lips parted. Images flashed through his impaired brain, and he couldn't decide which he wanted more – to shove his cock past those soft lips, or lick the sweat from her body, one inch at a time.

He stood silent, watching her breathe, almost afraid to breathe himself – afraid he'd wake and find it was a dream – a fantasy. He wasn't the man for her. He knew it in his soul, but it didn't keep his body from wanting her.

A wave of possessiveness stole over him. The erotic tableau was for him only. The tantalizing band of exposed skin was meant for his hands, his lips, and no other. Those lips were meant for his cock, his kiss. And the rest of her, the hot center taunting him in his dreams, that was his too, and he'd murder anyone who believed otherwise.

She stirred, turning those sapphire blue eyes on him. An invisible current flowed between them, releasing Dell from his paralysis. *Wrong.* What he wanted was so wrong, but like a bug drawn to the light, he couldn't overcome nature. Knowing he was courting the flames of hell, he closed the distance between them. Her gaze followed his progress until he joined her on the sofa.

"Dell," she breathed.

"Shh. Let me take care of you," he said. He bathed her face with the wet cloth, trailing the cool fabric across her forehead, her flushed cheeks, over her lips and down the length of her chin. Her chest rose and fell on a sigh as he dragged the cloth over her chest, pushing the edges of her blouse aside as he descended.

"You're so beautiful." He brushed the cloth over the swell of her breasts, pausing to watch a drop of water disappear into the cleft. He groaned and dipped his head.

Moth. Flame.

Caro gasped and arched her back as his tongue delved into the spot in search of the elusive water droplet. Her silk skin tasted of salt and the heat of her body magnified her scent. His nostrils flared.

Intoxicating.

He drew his tongue across the top of one lace-clad breast, then the other before he hooked his index finger in one cup. Her skin set him on fire. And when his questing digit found the hard nub he sought, her moan of pleasure shattered him.

Lost.

"I've got to see you, Caro," he said. He searched her eyes for resistance and saw need and a raw hunger that matched his own. Still, he vowed to himself to take it slow, savor every moment. Even though he saw acceptance now, if she changed her mind, he would stop, even if it killed him. She was too precious, too perfect, and he'd never do anything to harm her.

Mine.

He used his finger to draw the fabric down until her darkened areola peeked above the lace. He touched his tongue to the puckered skin before he dipped lower to taste the still hidden jewel. It was too much.

It wasn't enough.

He had to have more. He jerked the fabric, and at the same time sucked her nipple into his mouth, pulling hard on her sensitive skin. Suddenly, her hands cradled his head, her fingers combing through his hair, holding him to her. A sexy moan vibrated through her chest, setting him aflame.

Mine. Mine.

Then she was beneath him on the sofa. He feasted on one breast, while he fumbled with the back closure of her bra. It came loose and he pushed the fabric down to expose both breasts. He released her, pushing up to see the treasure he'd uncovered.

"My God, Carolina." He reverently touched one breast, testing the weight in his palm. He brushed his thumb across the tight nipple. "You are so damned perfect."

"Dell." His name was a whisper on her lips. He tore his eyes from her breasts. He saw wonder and surrender in her eyes. Something inside him shifted and he swallowed hard.

"Caro, my sweet Carolina."

"Love me, Dell."

He was hard as a post with want and need, but this was Carolina and hurting her wasn't an option. He would be a gentleman about this for her. "You don't know how much I want to, Caro." He ground his erection against her stomach to emphasize the point. "Are you sure this is what you want?"

"Please, Dell." Her hips rose to meet his. "Don't make me beg."

"Ah, sweet Carolina, you'll never have to beg."

She squealed as he swept her into his arms and carried her to the back of the coach, laying her on his bed. He stripped and came down beside her. With a measure of control he didn't know he was capable of, he stripped her clothes from her, one garment at a time, indulging in his fantasy of licking the perspiration from her, one inch at a time.

Caro moaned and squirmed beneath his ministrations. He touched, he tasted, he worshipped, and then he wedged his shoulders between her thighs and feasted.

No nectar on earth was sweeter than his Carolina, and she was his. He'd denied it enough, postponing his claim of her far too long.

Mine.

Her throaty moans, her fingers against his scalp drove him on. Her pleasure became his goal in life. Her thighs pillowed his face. Her scent, her taste became a part of him. She was close, he could feel the tension building as his tongue stroked inside her. He needed her climax more than he needed his own, and he was beyond desperate.

Sweet Carolina

Timing was something he understood. He waited, assessed, calculated. He was in the driver's seat – evaluating every sound, every motion from her writhing body in order to coax optimum performance from her. He used all his senses to know when she needed him to throttle up, and in that instant, he plunged two fingers deep inside her and clamped his teeth over her clit while his tongue flicked over the captured nub. She shattered, her body convulsing in a jagged rhythm in tempo with his heartbeat. Liquid heat bathed his face and hand. His head spun as he absorbed her climax into his psyche. Nothing would ever be better than this, he thought.

She curled into him, sated and smiling. He held her in a gentle, yet firm, embrace until her breathing calmed. Her skin was satin beneath his fingers as he learned the curve of her back, the swell of her hips and her sweet ass. All this was his, but he needed more. He needed all of her.

"Caro," he said as he felt her smile against his chest. His cock twitched against her stomach.

"Mmm," she murmured. She pressed a kiss to his heated skin. Flames licked at his insides.

"We're not through," he said.

Her hand on his stomach slipped lower. His body tensed in anticipation. Her fingers found his erection, closing around him like a velvet vise. Air swooshed from his lungs and he bucked, sucking in a ragged breath. "Sweet Jesus, Carolina." He called on every bit of restraint to allow her to explore. It was the least he could do before he claimed her final prize. "You're killing me, sweetheart."

She rolled away from him, keeping his cock prisoner to her inquisitive hand so all he could do was roll with her until she was beneath him, guiding his cock to her entrance. Her heat called to him. He craved it more than he'd ever craved anything in his life. In a moment of sanity, he braked. "Protection." His voice sounded like gravel.

"Hurry," she said.

Dell leaned over, stretching to reach the drawer in the nightstand, keeping her pinned beneath his hips while praying he'd find a condom in there. Track bunnies weren't his style, but he'd been desperate a time or two. But never like this. Never to the point where death looked better than the prospect of having to stop now. He silently cursed as he ran his fingers across the bottom of the drawer and came up empty.

87

Hell.

"Well, shit." He scrambled off her to sit on the edge of the bed. He jerked the drawer completely out of its mounting and began tossing random things to the floor.

"No fire suit?" she asked.

"I won't take no for an answer. There has to be one in here somewhere." One lonely foil package caught his eye and he breathed a shaky sigh of relief. "Thank God."

Caro's sweet smile and the sparkle in her eyes told him she was as relieved as he. He suited up and slid between her welcoming thighs.

"Are you sure, Carolina?"

Her hips rose and fell. "Yes, I'm sure."

He held himself above her on his forearms, cradling her face in his hands. His thumbs stroked her cheekbones, now flushed with desire. Her earlier humor was gone, replaced by a tender invitation. "I can't wait any longer, Carolina."

"Don't," she whispered.

He claimed her mouth and her core in tandem.

Heaven.

She was hot and tight, and so damned wet he almost lost it. He nudged deeper and she let out a startled gasp. He used the opportunity to thrust his tongue past her lips, doing with it what he couldn't risk doing with his cock. Not yet. He would not go off like a teenager with his first girl. He wanted to make this last – forever.

Caro returned his kiss, sucking his tongue, dueling and moaning low in her throat. Finally, he could take no more. He jerked his mouth from hers. "Oh fuck!"

He moved, pulling out and plunging back in. Hard. Fast. Finesse and rhythm were beyond him. Nothing had ever felt this good, this right, this perfect. "Oh God, Carolina," he clenched his jaw and rose above her, his hands braced either side of her shoulders. He dared to look at her. Her breasts bounced with each thrust. Her lips were swollen and wet from his kisses. In the back of his mind, he registered her legs anchored around his hips, her fingernails clinging to his back. And in her eyes, he saw a love he didn't deserve.

"Dell," she breathed.

"Come for me, Caro."

A few more strokes and her body tensed. She drew her head back, exposing her neck to him. He bent, took a gentle bite, palming one breast. He arched his back, took the perfect mound into his mouth and sucked the nipple hard.

She exploded beneath him. Dell released her breast, rose above her and throwing his head back, he rode her hard. Need drove him. Her body held him prisoner, claiming him as surely as he claimed her.

His balls clenched tight. Sparks erupted in the small of his back and shot like a flash-fire through his groin. He came in great, heaving spurts that seemed to drain the very life from him. The pain was so sharp, it almost took him under, and would have if the pleasure hadn't been equal to it.

"God almighty," he swore as he collapsed on top of her. "Sweet, God almighty."

Hell.

Chapter Eleven

What the hell had he done?

The muted sound of water sluicing down the drain did nothing to calm him. He envied every droplet now sliding down Caro's naked body and wished the tiny shower were big enough for two. The reality of Caro was more than he dreamed, and every bit a nightmare. Now that he'd had her, he couldn't give her up, but he couldn't keep her either. The world they lived in was too small to keep a relationship a secret, and if Caro were going to have any credibility as an owner, the rumors about them had to stay rumors.

The water cut off and Dell grabbed a pair of jeans from the built-in dresser and pulled them on commando-style. Another drawer yielded a faded T-shirt he hastily pulled on. He congratulated himself on his restraint as he passed the bathroom door without stopping on his way to the front of the coach. Mindless of the time of day, he pulled a beer from the refrigerator and downed half of it in one pull.

Focus. He needed to pull his head out of his ass and think. He had one goal – to win, and if he could take Warner out in the process, so much the better. Caro had nothing to do with anything. She was a means to a goal. A ride. He smiled at the pun. Yeah, she was quite the ride, everything a man needed, soft, warm, responsive. And for those glorious moments when he made love to her, he hadn't thought of anything but her and driving his cock into her mind-blowing heat.

But he'd do well to remember she was his ride – professionally. Without her, there was no racing, and the track was the only place he had any business looking for satisfaction. No more Caro.

The bathroom door opened and closed and Dell turned to see Caro striding up the narrow hallway toward him. She'd dressed in the clothes she came in, but now her hair was damp and the clothes a bit more wrinkled than normal wear could account for. Her cheeks glowed and her eyes sparkled. Her lips were swollen he noted, and she wore no makeup. She looked well fucked.

Fuck it. His resolve blew a gasket. Who was he kidding? He wasn't giving Caro up. They'd have to be discreet. He could do discreet. She could come to his place, or better yet, he'd go to hers. He'd buy a plain car – something that wouldn't attract attention parked in her driveway – something he normally wouldn't be caught dead in.

She stopped just out of his reach. She'd finally come to her senses in the shower. As she stood there staring at Dell, knowing in intimate detail what was hidden beneath those sexy as hell tight jeans and T-shirt, she wondered why her good sense couldn't have made an appearance when she really needed it – before she begged Dell Wayne to make love to her. And she had begged. That was something she wouldn't soon forget. Just like the feel of his hands, and his lips, and...well, she shouldn't go there again.

"This was a mistake," she said.

Dell smiled and reached for her. She took a step back and held her hand up in a signal every idiot understood. Dell, thankfully, retreated. "Caro. Don't try to tell me it wasn't good."

Oh lord! The smug son-of-a-bitch would cut straight to the chase. Caro squared her shoulders and took a deep breath before answering.

"No. I won't lie, Dell. I had a good time – the best time, actually, but it was wrong." She brushed past him to the door. She paused with her hand on the latch and turned to him. It took her until the hot water ran out to come up with an excuse, and it was a darn good one, if she did say so herself.

"You know how small this world is, and how AARA is all about family values. If anyone found out...well, I'd be ruined." As soon as the words were out of her mouth, she high-tailed it out of there, half expecting him to try to stop her, and half wishing he would.

Caro glanced around as she made her way out of Dell's motor coach. Relieved to see no one, she hurried across the campground toward the parking area where she'd left her car. Normally, she would have flagged down one of the track volunteers buzzing around in golf carts to take her out to the remote lot, but not today. She couldn't risk someone seeing and commenting on the state of her hair or her clothes. It wouldn't take a genius to figure out how she'd gotten this way. Whether they put two and two together to come up with Dell and her, it didn't matter. All that would matter was the equation. One variable was as bad as any other when it came to whom she slept with. That it happened at the track would only make it worse if anyone found out.

Dell let her go. What choice did he have? She was right. Her reputation had to be above reproach in this business or the other owners would force her out, maybe AARA itself. On the other hand, he'd get slaps on the back and brownie points for screwing the boss. It wasn't fair, but that's the way things were around the track. Wasn't his dad's life proof enough? Caudell Senior slept with every track bunny who hopped into his line of vision, and he'd basked in the sunshine of masculine approval because of it.

"Well, fuck," Dell said, tossing his now empty beer bottle into the wastebasket.

❧

Her lady parts were still throbbing from Dell's attentions the next day when she set out for the owner's meeting. She checked and double-checked her appearance before leaving the hauler, as if she expected to find a big red letter "A" on her forehead. Assured she looked normal, as normal as any woman could in a roomful of mostly middle-aged men, she pushed the door open and stepped inside. Heads turned as she made her way as close to the front as possible. Her size put her at a disadvantage among the men who were her counterparts, but she refused to be intimidated. She was one of them, and they'd better get used to it.

Caro acknowledged a few of the other owners who spoke to her and waved at another across the room. Butch Renfro stood on the opposite side. She caught his eye and inclined her head in a polite, but not exactly friendly greeting. He smirked, then turned his attention to the man on his left. Caro inwardly shrugged; certain now Russell had delivered her message. She wasn't going to sell. Not unless there was no other option. She refused to dwell on how soon it might come to fruition.

The meeting was as boring as ever and Caro found it difficult to concentrate on the agenda. Snippets of her time in Dell's bed kept creeping in, stealing her thoughts. Finally, the meeting was over. Caro waited her turn to file out the single door. Being near the front, she was one of the last to leave. She stepped out to find Butch Renfro waiting for her.

"Ms. Hawkins," he said. "Do you have a minute?"

Caro kept walking. "No, I'm afraid I don't." Butch settled in beside her. "Besides, we don't have anything to discuss. I'm not selling."

"I admire your spunk, Carolina, but you and I both know this isn't any place for a woman. Your daddy knew it too. He must be turning over in his grave to see you dressed like that, hanging out with grease monkeys and the like."

Caro seethed at his chastising tone and picked up the pace, hoping he'd get the message and move on. When he continued to dog her steps, she stopped and turned to him. "Look, Mr. Renfro, I have no plans to sell, not to you or anyone else. You can insult my fashion choices all you want, but I'm not stupid enough to sit in the pit wearing anything other than a fire suit. As for my father, he had an antiquated viewpoint regarding a woman's place in this world, but I loved him anyway. Maybe he didn't want this life for me, but I aim to make him proud, and I'm going to do it by associating with some of the most talented and best-educated people I can. Just in case you don't know who I'm talking about, those are the people you erroneously refer to as grease monkeys." She turned. "Now, if you'll excuse me, I have a lot to do before they wave the green flag."

She instantly put Renfro out of her mind when she strode into the garage – right into the middle of chaos. Dell's car had already been taken out for inspection. Instead of setting up their work area, her entire pit crew stood around, shouting at each other over the roar of engines on either side of their assigned stall. "What's going on?" she asked, raising her voice to be heard. Everyone stopped yelling and half a dozen heads turned her way.

"Nothing, Ms. Hawkins." This from the catch can man, and the youngest member of the pit crew.

"Everything's under control, Caro," Russell said.

Caro eyed the silent group, uncertain whether she should ask more questions, or let the situation, whatever it was, resolve itself. They'd clammed up fast enough, which told her it was probably one of those inexplicable guy things – of which she'd already had plenty of for one day. "Okay, but we don't have time for this. The race starts in less than an hour." She catalogued the faces and realized Dell wasn't among them. "Where's our driver?"

"He's already gone out for the driver introductions and interviews," Russell said. Caro nodded.

"Good." At least someone was doing his job. "Let's get a move on. I know the pit stops are scheduled in the All-Star race, but we still need to be on our toes. No messing around. Dell needs to win at least one of the heats."

She left to a chorus of "Yes, ma'ams." After a stop in the hauler for her notebook, Caro made her way to their assigned pit stall. She had her foot on the first rung of the war wagon when an arm snaked around her waist, pulling her back, and over the wall onto the track.

"Stand with me," Dell said in her ear as he dropped her feet to the ground. "I don't want to be out here all alone."

Caro turned and frowned at him. "You could have just asked," she said, smoothing imaginary wrinkles out of her fire suit.

"You wouldn't have come," he said. "I know you." He placed a hand on the small of her back, gently turning her and compelling her to walk beside him. She complied rather than put up a fight to draw even more attention. "All the other owners are out here for the national anthem, you should be too."

"The other owners aren't me," she said.

Dell dipped his head close to hers. "What you mean is, the other owners aren't sleeping with their drivers," he said. Her skin flushed with heat and it had nothing to do with the sun beating down on them. Dell's next words knocked her completely off balance. "But you don't know that for sure."

Caro laughed the rest of the way to Dell's car where he arranged her so they stood hip-to-hip, facing the flagpole. She was vaguely aware of cameras snapping around them, but Dell's ridiculous statement drained the tension from her body. He was right. There was nothing wrong with her standing with her driver during the pre-race festivities, Caro rationalized. So what if the spot she occupied was traditionally filled by wives and girlfriends – or husbands in rare cases. Some of the younger drivers invited their mothers to fill the spot.

The ceremony came to an end, and Caro turned to wish Dell good luck. Before the words were out, he snaked an arm around her and brought her flush against his hard body. She instantly stiffened and tried to push away, but he held her tight. She looked up at him, a protest on her lips. Dell kissed her. Right in front of God and the elite of AARA. Her first instinct was to get away, but it lasted the span of one record lap around the track, no more, and then she kissed him back.

As quickly as he grabbed her, he let her go. With a knowing smile, he hoisted himself through the car window and into the driver's seat. Caro watched in muted shock as he settled in and reached for his helmet. He paused, holding his helmet in his hands, and winked at her. "Wish me luck," he said.

Caro fumed. The sparks flying off her could have fired the engines on half the cars lined up to take the track. She took a step back as Dell heeded the order to start the engine. The roar of fifty high performance engines firing at the same time drowned out whatever retort her sizzled brain might have come up with, provided her brain was actually functioning – which it was not. The ground trembled beneath her feet, reminding her it was time to leave. Dell smiled at her, and with a flick of his fingers, shooed her away.

◈

Dell fired the engine and called himself all kinds of an idiot. He didn't know what came over him. One minute he was immersed in pre-race musings regarding strategy in a winner-take-all race like this one, and the next, he was sweeping Caro off her feet, and all because he'd caught a glimpse of her fire suit-clad ass. Hauling her out on the track to stand beside him wasn't so bad. He'd told the truth. Most of the owners were out there, so there wasn't any reason she shouldn't be too.

What he hadn't expected was the way it felt to have her standing beside him – like he was some sort of gladiator and she was his woman. He made her laugh, and that made him ridiculously happy for some reason. She didn't laugh near enough these days. The Caro he remembered from their shared childhood laughed all the time. The sound of her laughter was like sunshine on the cold, dark places in his soul, and when it was time to send her on her way, he couldn't not kiss her.

Her body language screamed at him to stop, and he was going to, but something shifted and she went all soft in his arms, kissing him back. God almighty, he was a knight in shining armor going to battle to defend the damsel in distress. It took all his strength to step away from her, and he soon found out folding himself into the seat with a hard-on was no picnic either.

Damn. He needed to concentrate. With a million dollars at stake in the All-Star race, everyone took it seriously. He'd be a fool not to. He waved her away and dragged his thoughts back to where they belonged. Just because he was hell-bent on giving away his inheritance didn't mean he wanted to live the life of a pauper. He needed money of his own, and a million dollars would go a long way toward his goal of living off his own winnings rather than his father's.

The first twenty laps went without incident. The car handled well so he decided to skip the first optional pit stop in favor of possibly gaining track position. He'd love to win a million dollars, but there was a bonus purse for the winner of each twenty-lap segment too. Winning at least one would be good – preferably the last one. That would set him up as one of the first four to take the track after the mandatory pit stop before the final segment.

He pitted after forty laps, took four new tires, and managed to maintain decent track position. Going into the final twenty-lap segment, Dell was in decent position to make a run for the lead. He squeezed past the last three cars between him and the race leader without incident, leaving him with a clear view of the lead car's bumper.

"Drop low in turn two," his spotter advised.

"Roger that," Dell said. It was a sound strategy. Stater had taken the high groove on that turn the entire race, so if Dell kept his car in the low groove, he should be able to slip underneath and take the lead.

Dell bided his time. He only needed to be in the lead for the last lap – that was the only one that counted. Fifteen laps in, he made his move. Stater went high. Dell slid low and throttled up as much as he dared. It wasn't enough. Stater came out of the turn, throttled up a fraction of a second earlier than Dell and slipped back down in front of Dell on the backstretch.

Dell cursed and nosed up on Stater's bumper – fair warning he meant business. Stater took the warning to heart, and Dell made three more futile attempts to arrest the lead. With two laps to go, Dell threw caution to the wind.

"Don't do anything stupid," Caro warned through his headset.

Dell acknowledged her warning with one of his own. "Who's driving this car?" he asked as he cut deep and low, throttling up when reason cautioned to do the opposite. His opponent hesitated, no doubt taken by surprise at Dell's audacity. Stater recovered, recognized Dell's reckless bid and edged down the track until his rear bumper was within inches of clearing the front of Dell's car.

It was now or never. Dell pushed his car to the limit, calling Stater's bluff. The two cars jockeyed for the lead through the backstretch into turns three and four. Dell held his ground in the high-speed game of chicken. Coming out of turn four, Stater dropped low, bumping Dell onto the apron. Dell gripped the wheel tightly and retaliated by swinging back onto the track, right into the driver's side of Stater's car.

Metal ground against metal as the two cars rubbed along the front stretch toward the finish line. All he needed was an inch. A one-inch clearance to win this segment and be one of the top four in the final segment. Dell glanced to his right, but couldn't see Stater clearly. He calculated the distance in his mind and counted down silently. When he reached zero, he jerked the wheel left to disengage from the other car, and in the same instant, he throttled up. Stater did the same, but a fraction of a second too late. Dell shot forward, crossing the finish line ahead of Stater by six inches.

Dell immediately throttled down and watched as Stater shot him the finger as he sailed past him. None of it mattered now. He had the purse for winning the fourth segment, and he'd start in fourth position for the final ten-lap showdown.

"Shit, good driving, Dell," Jeff said. "Bring her in for the mandatory pit stop."

"Coming in," Dell said as he took a cool down lap before turning onto pit row. He came to a stop in their designated stall. The crew rushed to do their job, readying the car to go back out for the last segment. He'd start fourth, ahead of what remained of the fifty cars that began the race. With a million at stake, everyone was pushing it, taking risks they normally wouldn't, and as a result, the final field would be about twenty-five cars. Of those, few had any chance of winning, but it wouldn't stop them from trying. With that much cash on the line, even the sanest of drivers could go a little nuts.

Some of the drivers elected to stretch their legs during the ten-minute stop, but Dell stayed in the car. That didn't stop the reporters from jabbing microphones and cameras in the window. He expected the questions after the way he took the segment lead away from Stater, who was now regulated to one of the twenty or so also-rans starting in the back of the pack. Dell answered their questions, ignoring the way they tried to get his reaction to his Madman nickname.

The reporters got their sound bites and moved on to someone else. Dell focused on the final laps. This is where the gloves came off. The four winners of the previous segments would duel it out for the prize money. This was pure racing. No rules. Just drive, and do it better than the other three. Dell fired the engine on cue and took his place in the second row, behind the pace car. Two laps around, the pace car would drop out, and the green flag would fly.

"Go get 'em!" His spotter's unnecessary words echoed Dell's thoughts as he throttled up and easily moved into third. The first and second place cars widened the gap, but Dell was on a mission to win. He closed the gap, but the drivers were running two-wide to prevent him from making a move. Dell counted down the laps in his head as he kept pace with the neck-and-neck leaders. Both cars belonged to the same owner, a man known for the nasty tactics he encouraged his drivers to employ on the track.

Dell cursed as they cut off his next bid for the lead. He backed off and settled in behind the pair for another lap. They came into turn four and Dell eased up on the bumper of the low car.

"Careful," Russell cautioned. "Those two aren't gonna to give you an inch."

"Fuck them," Dell said and tapped his grill against the lead car's bumper again. This was fucked up bullshit. It was obvious he had the faster car. They teamed up to shut him out, but he wasn't going to let them get away with it.

"Don't do anything stupid, Dell." Caro's voice came through his headset.

"Winning isn't stupid," he said as he gave the lead car another nudge, forcing both cars toward the wall, creating a gap on the inside. Dell cut left, slipping down the track on the front stretch into turn one. His combatants closed the gap, cutting him off once again.

Dell could taste the win. Could see the checkered flag come down as he crossed the finish line in the lead. No one was going to snatch it from him and get away with it.

Two laps to go.

He made one more bid for the lead and they cut him off again.

"So that's the way you want to play it," he muttered to himself. They weren't going to give him track position, so he'd take what was his, and be damned the consequences. If he wasn't going to win, they weren't either.

Dell drove under the white flag. One more lap. They thought they had it won, but Dell wasn't ready to concede the race. They rode high in turn one and Dell punched the nose of his car alongside them on the inside.

"Three wide," his spotter said.

No shit.

They realized their mistake and in turn two, they crowded him onto the apron. Dell crowded right back, grinding against the closest car – forcing him and his partner in the conspiracy to go high.

"Three wide!" his spotter yelled in his ear.

The cars bumped and rubbed through the backstretch into turn three. They forced Dell back to the apron in the turn, hitting him with a solid bump intended to take him out of the race. Dell countered with a quick jerk of the wheel, sending them all careening toward the wall.

"Dell!" Caro's voice.

"Fuck," he said as the outside car hit the wall first. Like boxcars on a runaway train, the second car followed the first in a shower of sparks and grinding metal. Dell glimpsed clear track ahead, then a cloud of smoke obscured his vision.

"Fuck, fuck, fuck!"

The impact rattled his teeth, then he was spinning inside the cloud. Crumpling metal and screeching tires added to the surreal tableau. He caught glimpses of bright colors interspersed with showers of sparks as he spun. Another jolt knocked the breath from his lungs. His body slammed against the restraint and back against the seat. He was weightless. Then the world tumbled in a kaleidoscope of colors, some bright, some dark and all accompanied by the devil's orchestra.

In the back of his mind, he understood what was happening, but he was helpless to stop it. He was nothing more than an ant in a tin can being kicked down the street by a giant.

He heard voices, but couldn't make out what they were saying. He shook his head to clear the ringing in his ears. His head pounded and his shoulders ached where the restraints bit into them. Too tight, he thought, wondering how it got that way. It wasn't too tight when he started the race.

Dell opened his eyes. His world was upside down. He shook his head again and still his world was upside down. He swatted at the hand trying to unhook his restraint. No. *Can't take it off.*

"Easy man. We'll get you out. Just take it easy."

Dell turned toward the man speaking. His head spun with the effort to make sense of the helmeted head poking upside down through his window. Dell reached for his own helmet and fumbled with the fastener. A gloved hand grabbed his wrist.

"Leave it on, Dell. We'll have you out in a minute. Let us do the work."

Dell mumbled something in response, then his world went black.

Chapter Twelve

Time slowed to a crawl and Caro watched in horror as the scene played out before her. She'd seen plenty of crashes, but none as violent as this one. And Dell was right in the middle of it. Her stomach lurched and her lungs ceased as the mass of twisted, grinding metal encased in smoke, sparks, and the occasional flame careened around turn four and came to an eerily silent stop on the grass buffer between the track and pit road.

"Oh God, oh God, oh God," she chanted. "Dell," she shouted into the microphone. "Dell!"

Russell put a hand on her arm, momentarily drawing her attention away from the horrific scene on the track. "Give him a minute, Caro. He'll be okay, you'll see."

No, she didn't see. Emergency crews were on the scene almost before the mass of metal came to a complete stop, but it did nothing to ease her anxiety. A cloud of smoke obscured her vision. A lone figure emerged in a clear spot, only to be swallowed up again by the smoke. Caro's heart skipped a beat. She realized the man swaggering out of the acrid mist wasn't Dell and her heart stopped completely.

"Where is he?" she asked. "Why isn't he out of the car?" She thumbed the communication button again. "Dell! Answer me, goddamn you!"

"Caro, calm down. Give the boy some time."

"Time?" She stood and yanked her headset off, throwing it across the war wagon. It hit the other side of the desk and recoiled as it came to the end of its tether. "He's had plenty of time," she said. "How freakin' long does it take to get out of a car?"

101

Too long, her analytical brain told her. It was taking too long. Something was wrong. He couldn't get out. She had to help him. "I'm going down there."

"Caro, wait," Russell called after her, but she was down the ladder, heading for the break in the wall.

"You can't go out there, ma'am." The burly guard wearing a yellow windbreaker with the word, "Security," emblazoned on it, stopped her before she got her leg over the wall.

"That's my driver out there," she said by way of explanation.

"I don't care who it is, you aren't going past this point. Let the emergency folks do their job."

Caro scanned the wreckage. The undercarriage of one car stuck up, one tire spinning, the other three nothing more than ragged strips of torn rubber. A man wearing the telltale, red fire suit of a track medic lay on the ground on the driver's side, his body half in, half out of the driver's window. Caro swallowed the bile rising in her throat.

Dell. Dell was inside that car. She pointed a shaky finger in the direction of the crumpled wreckage. "That's my car. I own it. Dell drives for me."

The security guy looked in the direction she pointed. "I understand, ma'am, but I still can't let you onto the track."

"Please," she begged.

He sighed and she swung her leg over the barrier again only to sail back over it in the next instant. Wrapped in strong, yellow-clad arms, she wasn't going anywhere.

"Look, lady, if you promise not to make a run for it again, I'll take you over to where the ambulance will come through. You can wait there. I'll try to find out what I can for you. Okay?"

Caro looked over her shoulder and nodded. "Okay. Let's go." She wiggled and he released her. Then, grabbing her bicep in a vise-like grip, he force-marched her to a gap in the wall.

"Wait here," he said, looking her in the eye until he gained her agreement. She watched helplessly as he headed toward the wreckage.

She'd never prayed so hard in her life as she did during the minutes she waited for the guard to return with news. If Dell were dead…

No. He couldn't be, because she was going to kill him. She held onto her anger, refusing to believe she wouldn't have the chance to unleash it on Dell. He had to be alive. She wouldn't accept anything else.

Minutes ticked by and her world narrowed to what she could see of the car. The medic on the scene obscured her view. He was still half inside the car. That was good, wasn't it? If Dell were dead, there wouldn't be any reason to still be there. He'd move on to someone he could help. No use wasting time on a dead man.

Please. Please. Please. The mantra repeated in her head. *I love you, Dell. Don't you dare die on me now.* She didn't question the strength of her feelings. She'd known for some time now she was in love with Dell. There was nothing comforting about the knowledge, so she'd ignored it, except for yesterday when she'd let her stupid emotions get the best of her.

Dell wasn't the kind of man a woman could count on. He lived only for himself with little or no care for others. And for whatever reason, he courted death every time he got inside a race car. No, he wasn't the kind of man she should give her heart to, but damn it, her heart wouldn't listen to reason.

Caro chewed her lower lip as the security guard spoke with the medics. He turned, pointing in her direction. Several sets of eyes looked her way, then the knot of men put their heads together.

Please. Please. Please.

An eternity later, the guard returned. Her whole body shook with dread. Caro folded her arms around her mid-section and locked her knees so she wouldn't fall. "Well?" she asked as he got within hearing range.

"He's alive. That's about all they know. They said there wasn't much blood."

"That's good, right?"

"Could be. Could be internal injuries. They said he blacked out right after they showed up. Hasn't come to yet."

"Oh God, oh God, oh God."

"Look, lady, he's probably going to be alright. They said he most likely passed out from hanging upside down – that's all. They're doing everything by the book. They'll get him out, but they have to be careful not to make things worse."

Caro nodded in understanding, not trusting her voice beyond single syllables. The guard put both his big hands on her shoulders and turned her toward the wreckage. "See? They've got him out already."

"Oh God, oh God, oh God," she prayed. *Please let him be okay.*

❧

Roz Lee

More voices, hushed this time. Not like the others he remembered – some shouting orders, another one – calm and confident telling him to let them do the work. What work? Dell forced one eyelid open a tiny crack. Bright lights. He was cold. Still. Dead?

He shifted his legs. Pain. Not awful, but enough to tell him he wasn't dead. Dead people didn't feel, did they?

"Dell." Caro's voice. "Dell, you're okay. You're going to be okay," she said though there wasn't much conviction in her words. She sounded a bit shaky to him. He wanted to assure her, but he wasn't positive there were assurances to be made.

He tried to smile, but he couldn't be sure if his facial muscles followed orders or not. He tried to raise his hand to get her attention, but like his face, he wasn't sure anything moved. Someone squeezed his hand. He squeezed back. Caro. He'd know her touch anywhere. He smiled again, not knowing if he smiled for anyone besides himself.

"Dell," she coaxed. "You're going to be fine. Rest." She held his hand in hers, patting the back with her other hand. "Get better."

Her breath brushed across his ear in a soft caress. Were those her lips on his cheek? Maybe he imagined her kiss. He didn't care. If it were a dream, it was a good one. "I love you," the dream whispered in his ear.

※※

"Wake up so I can kill you, you arrogant, self-centered, suicidal idiot."

She was going to kill him – as soon as he was awake and able to understand what was happening to him.

Caro swiped the moisture from her cheeks with trembling fingers. God damn him all to hell for making her love him.

He lay so still, she caught herself leaning up from her chair beside his hospital bed, checking to make sure he was still breathing. Of course he was. They'd only sedated him to keep him still while they assessed the damage. They said he was belligerent when they brought him in, insisting he was fine.

In truth, he wasn't hurt all that bad. A few bruised ribs from the where he slammed against the restraint system, and his left arm was badly bruised, probably from being caught between the door panel and the driver's seat. He was damned lucky. Caro closed her eyes and sniffed back another bout of tears.

Damn. This wasn't fair. She wasn't supposed to fall for a driver, especially one hell-bent on destroying himself and her company in the process.

A knock on the door jolted her to attention. She dried her eyes again and sat up straighter. The door opened a few inches and Caro's shoulders slumped. "What are you doing here?" she asked.

"How is he?" Butch Renfro pushed the door partially open and stood with half his body in, the other half hidden by the door, as if he might need to dart behind it as a shield at any moment.

"Alive," she said. "I'm surprised you care."

He had the grace to look chagrined. "I'm sorry about what happened. Warner said he couldn't avoid hitting him. You know how it is, one minute you're fine, the next..."

"Yeah, I know. Who won, anyway?"

"Petersen. Can you believe it? He went from nineteenth to first in a matter of seconds. The kid did okay, avoided every crash of the night, and came out the winner."

Caro nodded her head. Sammy Petersen drove for one of the smaller garages with few sponsors. They could use the money. "Lucky."

"Yeah." He looked at his feet, glancing toward the still figure in the bed, then to Caro. "Can I see you outside for a minute?"

The last thing she wanted to do was talk to Butch Renfro, but the time had come to consider his offer. Why else would he be here? Hawkins Racing was as good as dead on the side of the road – it was only natural Renfro would drive by to see what parts he could strip before she was able to find a tow truck. If there were such a thing. She'd been too worried about Dell to run the numbers in her head, but his stunt today may have spun the last lug nut off.

She glanced at Dell to make sure he was still sleeping before she joined Renfro in the hall. "Make it quick, I need to get back in there in case he wakes up."

"I'm not going to beat around the bush, Carolina. You and I both know Hawkins Racing is on its last lap. In fact, today's crash may have done you in for good. Your daddy was a good friend. I'd hate to see the doors close on his legacy, so I'm offering to buy you out."

It was exactly what Caro expected, but she wasn't ready to give in yet. "I'll think about it," she said, and turned to go back to Dell.

Renfro's next words stopped her. She didn't bother to look at him as he delivered his coup de grace.

"Hawkins won't survive this, Carolina. Before I came over, I heard talk that AARA is going to hand down a big fine for Dell's part in this, and rumor has it they're going to park you for at least a couple of races."

Caro resisted the urge to rest her forehead on the door and weep. She'd cried enough today, she wouldn't let Renfro have the satisfaction of knowing he'd broken her. "They'll do what they think is right. Thanks for the warning." She pushed the door open, leaving him standing in the hall. She pressed her back against the door and closed her eyes.

"Caro?"

She jumped at the sound of his voice. "Dell!"

"What's the matter?" he asked. He didn't know how long he'd been out. Hours? Days? But Caro was still in her fire suit. Battered and bruised, his dick still reacted in predictable ways. Something to be thankful for, he mused as she crossed to his bedside.

"Hey, you're awake. How do you feel?"

He closed his eyes and groaned. "Like I got hit by about a dozen cars?"

"It's a bit of an exaggeration, but not by much," she said. "I guess if you can joke about it, you aren't hurting too bad."

"I'll live," he said, trying to sit up. He winced at the pain in his ribs and dropped back to the mattress, grabbing his ribcage with his good arm. "Son of a bitch!"

Caro's lips curled into a malicious smile. "Yeah, you might not want to move too fast for while. You have some bruised ribs, mostly on your left side. Nothing's broken though."

"Could have fooled me," he said, through clenched teeth.

Caro reached for the call button. "Now that you're awake, we can go home." She signaled for the nurse. "The doctor wanted to keep you overnight, but I told him you wouldn't want to stay."

"Thanks," he said, infusing the word with all the sarcasm he could muster.

"What? You want to stay here?"

"No," he barked, wincing again as his knee-jerk response earned another protest from his ribcage. "You're right. I want to go home. How soon can we get out of here?"

The duty nurse stepped in, and having heard Dell's question, she answered for Caro. "You can leave in a few minutes, Mr. Wayne. I need to check your vital signs. I'll have the business office send someone up with your paperwork. As soon as you sign on the dotted line, you're free to go." She checked this and that, and all the while Dell watched Caro flit about the room, gathering...stuff. He had no idea what, and didn't care. Her eyes were red and swollen as if she'd been crying. Shit. A memory, or was it a dream? flitted through his brain. Whispered words. Caro's voice telling him she loved him.

"Your heartbeat is elevated," the nurse said. Dell glanced at his wrist where the nurse pressed her latex-covered fingers to his pulse. He willed his heart to slow. It was Caro. She did that to him. He closed his eyes as the nurse silently counted his heartbeat again. This time, she dropped his wrist. "There, no problem. It's a little fast," she glanced at Caro who was engrossed in folding his fire suit and stuffing it into a plastic bag with the hospital logo on it, "but that's to be expected." She slapped a pressure cuff around his bicep and pumped it up until Dell's eyes bulged. When she was through, she winked at him. "You're good to go." She folded the cuff and replaced it in the basket on the wall above his head. "Under the circumstances, a little high blood pressure is probably a good thing," she said.

"Thanks," Dell said.

"No problem." She bent close and lowered her voice. "Don't crash this time. This race might be one you really ought to win," she said, then she patted him on the arm and left.

Right. Caro's whispered declaration, real or imagined, echoed through his brain. He didn't deserve a woman like Carolina. He had no business thinking of a future with her. She gave herself to him once, and then she said it was a mistake. Wasn't that the understatement of the year? But he couldn't quit thinking about her, or remembering the feel of her skin beneath him, enfolding him in her wholesome goodness.

She was everything a woman ought to be, and he was nothing a man should be. Hadn't his dad said it enough times? Caro deserved a winner, someone to stand beside her, someone to support her. He wasn't that man. He didn't know *how* to be that man. But it didn't stop him from wanting to try, as futile as the effort might be.

He congratulated himself for making it to her car in the parking lot without collapsing, but it was a near thing. Everything on him hurt, and whatever they'd given him for pain wore off long ago.

"We'll stop at a pharmacy and fill your prescription," Caro said as she drove down the ramp to the lower level of the parking structure.

"No, take me back to the track. Aspirin will do. I'll be good to go in time for practice runs this week."

"Look, Dell," she said. The hesitation in her voice compelled him to look at her rather than the road.

"What?" he asked.

"We may not have a car in the race this week. Butch Renfro stopped by. He said he'd heard rumors we may be parked for a few races."

"Parked? Are you kidding me?" He gingerly supported his aching ribs as he tried to turn to get a better look at her face.

"No, not kidding. He said there would be fines too. I've been with you, and my cell phone was off, so I don't know what's going on at the track, but Butch seemed to think it was foregone conclusion."

"Shit." Dell turned his attention back to the road. "We'll protest the decision," he said.

Caro sighed. Dell didn't like the sound of it, but he kept his mouth shut. They drove in silence to his place on Lake Norman. Caro pulled up in front of his house.

"Thanks for the ride," he said, bailing out of the car as quickly as possible given the state of his ribs. "I'll see you at the track."

Chapter Thirteen

Caro rubbed her eyes with the heels of her hands. No amount of eye torture was going to make the numbers come out any better. She'd left Dell at his house and driven straight to the track. She skirted the garages and bee-lined straight for the AARA hauler, knowing they preferred to hand down bad news in person.

Hours later, she was still sitting behind her desk at Hawkins Racing, trying to find some way to make the numbers add up to get back on the track. As Butch Renfro predicted, the team fine was substantial and handed out with a liberal dose of chauvinistic idiocy that made her blood boil. She'd stood quietly and accepted their decree, all the while biting the inside of her cheek to keep from telling them off.

"Caro?"

She jumped at the sound of Dell's voice. "What are you doing here? Shouldn't you be in bed?"

"I'm fine. A little bunged up, but I'm good to go," he said. He did look better, but from the careful way he carried himself from the doorway to the chair in front of her desk, he wasn't one hundred percent yet.

"I guess you heard?" she asked.

"About the fines? Yeah, I heard. We should protest, Caro. I don't care if they fine me, but the team? That's wrong. I made the decisions, no one else."

"That's not the way the officials see it. They think I can't control you, and they're right. I've got no business running a race team if I can't control my employees."

"They said that?"

"They weren't that nice about it, but yeah, that's what they said." *Among other things.*

Dell's eyes narrowed and a wrinkle appeared between his eyebrows. "What else did they say?" he asked.

Caro waved his question away. It didn't matter now. What was done, was done. Hawkins Racing was through, or at least it was with her behind the wheel. "Nothing, Dell. Let it go."

He leaned toward the desk, his eyes locked on hers. "Tell me, Caro. Tell me what they said."

"Really, it doesn't matter, Dell." She eased back in her chair and sighed. "I was going to come out to your house and tell you, but since you're here…"

"I've got a feeling I'm not going to like this," he said.

"Probably not," she agreed. "Hawkins Racing is through, Dell. I'm going to sell to Butch Renfro."

Dell jerked to his feet and paced to the door and back in long, angry strides. "What the hell for?" he asked, standing over her desk, glaring down at her as if she were nuts. "Tell me what they said, Caro. What would make you sell to a low-life like Renfro?"

"It's more than what they said, Dell. It's a financial decision. I was counting on the purse from at least one of the races this week, and since we've been fined, and parked… well…" He stood over her, still as a statue, and more gorgeous than any man had a right to be, waiting for her to pour out her private shame. Only he didn't know, couldn't know, how much she'd hidden all season long.

"Well?" he prompted.

"I don't have the cash to pay the fine, and make payroll, much less keep building cars at the rate we've been doing."

"And?" he asked. But how did he know there was more? Was it that obvious? "There's more. What did they say, Caro?"

Oh, what did it matter? It wasn't like she was going to be able to keep it a secret anyway. Keeping secrets at a racetrack was like trying to keep water in a leaky radiator. You could patch the holes, but sooner or later, the whole thing would give, and all the water would come gushing out at once. "They know about us." She wagged her finger, indicating Dell and herself. "They know about what we did, or at least they suspect."

"So?"

Could he be that dense? "So, someone saw me leaving your coach the other day and did the math. It added up to you and me, well, you know. Anyway, word got back to the officials..."

"Are you friggin' kidding me?" Dell stomped back to the door and returned to plop down in the chair he'd vacated earlier and run his hands through his hair. "That's what the team fine is for, isn't it?"

Caro nodded. "Yes."

"They can't do it. It's none of their business what we do behind closed doors."

"It is if I walk across the infield looking like I've been... well, like I just crawled out of bed. And, there are pictures."

"What pictures?"

"Apparently, female owners aren't allowed to kiss their driver's before a race," she said, sliding a piece of paper across her desk to him.

Dell took the screen shot taken from a popular racing website and studied it before dropping it back on her desk. His hair stood on end where he raked his fingers through it, and the line between his eyebrows was now a deep furrow. "I'll pay the fine."

Caro shook her head. "I can't let you pay my fine, Dell."

"Why the hell not? I was there too."

"Yes, you were, but they don't fine men for immoral behavior, only women. They're probably ordering you a plaque right now."

She'd never seen Dell turn that shade of red before. He reminded her of a teakettle building up steam, ready to blow. She held up a staying hand. "I'm over it, Dell. I believed I could do this, run a team and be successful at it, but I guess my dad was right. This is no place for a woman. Renfro says he'll make this week's payroll if I agree to sell." She picked up a sheaf of papers and let them fall back to the desk. "I don't have much choice. I owe it to the employees to make sure they get paid. I can't let them down too."

Dell hated the look of defeat in her eyes. It did something to his insides, twisting them all up until he couldn't breathe. This was so wrong. Carolina, his sweet Carolina didn't deserve to lose her dream. And it was all his fault. If he'd kept his dick in his pants, there wouldn't be anything to talk about. She'd be above reproach. And damn, why hadn't he considered the financial drain he'd put on the team? He'd wrecked enough cars to fill a junkyard, and brought in very little purse money.

Whispered words echoed in his mind. Dream or reality? Did it matter which? Not in the least. It was stupid to dream she could love him, much less dream of accepting it if it were a reality. This was his fault. All of it – Caro's degradation because he seduced her – the fines – the bottom line. All his fault. He had to do something to fix it.

"Have you told Renfro your decision?"

"No. I wanted to tell my employees first."

"How much do you need?"

"Dell." She said his name like a yellow flag – caution. He ignored the warning as he had so many others.

"Tell me how much it'll take to keep the doors open, Caro."

She sighed and consulted a sheet of paper on her desk. After a while, she named a figure. Dell nodded. "And how much to finish the season?"

She shook her head. "I don't know, Dell. Let's not even go there. We're parked for this week and next, and without purse money…"

"I have purse money," he said. "I have more goddamned purse money than I know what to do with. I've tried giving it away, but it multiplies like rabbits. I might as well do something good with it. Let me help you, Caro. If you don't want me to give you the money, at least let me be a silent partner. I swear I won't tell you how to spend any of it." He held his hand up in some sort of scout salute – he thought.

"I can't let you do it, Dell. I've made a mess of things, and I'd hate myself even more if I took your money and lost it all too."

Dell watched her closely. He noticed the little spark of hope in her eyes when he mentioned being a silent partner, but it flared out quickly. There was something else she wasn't telling him. He was good with numbers, always had been. He did a quick mental calculation of the expenses versus the team's income since he'd come on board, and though the expenses outstripped the income, it shouldn't have been enough to put the team in such dire straits.

"How far in debt was the team when you took it over?" he asked. Bingo. Caro closed her eyes and sank back into her chair. He fuckin' hated the way her shoulders slumped in defeat and the resignation in her voice when she finally sat forward, folding her hands on the desk, and looked him in the eye.

"On a scale of one to ten? Eleven?"

Well, shit. What the hell had Stewart Hawkins been thinking? How could a man up and die and leave his failing company to a daughter he didn't want running it to begin with? What kind of man didn't make plans for that sort of thing? Dell held her gaze while he sorted out what he wanted to say. He couldn't fuck this up. Too many people had already stomped on Caro's pride – himself included. He needed to get this right the first time.

"The way I see it, you started out with the odds stacked against you. You took on debt that wasn't yours, you took on me, a liability by anyone's standards, and you're taking on the entire racing establishment all at one time. I can't do anything about the racing establishment, and I won't do anything about me. I won't quit, Caro. You can fire me, but we both know you won't find another Cup driver, at least not one who's willing to work for a percentage of winnings only." She opened her mouth to protest, but Dell held up his hand. "No, hear me out. I can amend my contract to reflect the new compensation arrangement, and I will. I can also pay off the debt you assumed when you took over Hawkins Racing."

He held up his hand to stop her one more time. "I believe in you, Caro. The engine you're working on is good, real good. We're parked for the next two weeks. Nothing we can do about that. Let me loan you the money to pay off the debt – at a low interest rate, say, zero percent, with no payment due until the end of the season. In the meantime, we use the next two weeks to work on the engine and build a new car or two, and when we're back on the track, I'll do everything I can to win."

Caro stared at him as if he'd lost his last marble, and perhaps he had. No matter what, he wouldn't let Caro lose her dream. Hell, he'd lost all of his long ago, and he didn't wish the same kind of pain on anyone.

"I'm giving you a chance to show the ol' boys' club what you can do, Caro. Show them the new Hawkins engine, and make them eat their words."

"But if you don't win, you'll go down with Hawkins Racing," she said.

"I'll win, Caro. I promise."

"Not if you drive like you've been driving. You're a menace on the track, Dell. What happened to the driver they used to say was going to change racing? He's the driver I wanted when I hired you. I was stupid and naïve. I thought that promising driver was in there

113

somewhere, that all I had to do was give him a new ride and he'd be grateful enough to come out of hiding. Where is that driver, Dell?"

"He's here." Dell thumped his chest with his fist. "He's right here." The heat of his conviction warmed the spot where his fist made contact with his chest, and spread through his body. The driver she spoke of still existed, and Dell was going to find him again. For Carolina. She was right, that driver was good, but Dell buried him along with Caudell in a futile effort to be the driver his father wanted him to be. Well, fuck that. Caudell only needed one son to follow in his footsteps, and as far as Dell was concerned, that honor belonged to Warner. Dell would never be the son Caudell wanted him to be, but he could be the man Caro needed, and perhaps, if he were really lucky, wanted too.

"Give me a chance to prove it, Caro. For the last three years, I've been trying to prove something to a dead man, but I've got something more important to prove. I want to prove I can be the man you need."

Caro grabbed a tissue from the box on the corner of her desk and dabbed at the corners of her eyes. Shit. He'd made her cry again.

"Don't cry, Caro." The words, I love you, nearly tumbled off the tip of his tongue, but he couldn't say them. He couldn't put that kind of shit in her lap too. "I've got the money. Truckloads of it. I believe in you. Take the money. Show the racing world who Caro Hawkins is, and I'll show you the driver you thought you hired. I promise."

A trickle of sweat slid down his spine as he sat with clenched fists awaiting Caro's decision. He was afraid to breathe, afraid any movement might call attention to his anxiety.

She rocked back in her chair and studied him with narrowed eyes. He didn't know what he would do if she said no. Probably beg. It wasn't out of the question.

At long last, Caro stood and walked to the bank of windows overlooking the garage. Dell followed her with his eyes as she crossed the room and flicked a switch beside the window. Light flooded the empty room. Dell unglued his ass from the chair and went to stand behind her. He wrapped his arms around her waist and tugged gently. She leaned into him, but remained stiff as if the tension in her body was the only thing holding her together. Her scent wafted over and through him, filling him with an emotion so foreign, it stole his breath.

He wanted to be the man she needed more than he wanted his next breath.

"I grew up in this garage," she said. Her hands closed over his. "I'm not ready to give it up, Dell."

"You don't have to. Let me help you."

"I don't know. It might just postpone the inevitable."

"The only thing you know for certain is if you sell to Renfro, Hawkins Racing will be done. He'll dismantle the shop, take what he wants for himself and leave the rest. That's a given. As long as you keep the doors open, there's a chance, Caro." He kissed the top of her head, then rested his chin there as they stared out at the empty shop. "Take the chance, Carolina. Even if you fail, you'll know you tried everything possible. No regrets."

She turned in his arms. Her eyes were bright with tears and uncertainty. Her palms rested over his heart and he wondered if she could feel its erratic beat. "No. No regrets, Dell." She sighed and seemed to melt in his arms. He cradled her close, stroking her back with one hand while the other held her cheek to his chest. God, she felt good in his arms, like she was meant to be there.

"We're going to do this, Caro. You and me. We're going to make Hawkins Racing a name to be reckoned with. You wait and see."

"Okay." The single word from her lips breathed life into his chest. He held her a moment longer, savoring the moment. He gently eased her away to look into her eyes.

"You won't regret this, Caro. I promise." To seal his promise, he pressed his lips to hers. The kiss was nothing more than a brush of lips before he tried to pull away. Her lashes fluttered down and she rose on tiptoe, her lips following his, halting his retreat.

"No regrets, Dell," she said. She pulled his head down to hers. Their lips met in a rush of longing and desperate need. She opened under him and his tongue swept in, claiming her soft heat to warm the dark recesses of his soul.

She tasted like the sweetest honey and he couldn't get enough. He took all she offered, and begged for more. Her lips promised carnal delights he wanted desperately to sample. He rocked his hips, pressing his erection against the soft pillow of her stomach. She groaned and molded her body to his.

Her hands found the hem of his shirt and slipped underneath. Her cool hands on his heated back almost brought him to his knees, but they also brought him to his senses.

"We can't," he said, disengaging from her and stepping back. He sucked in a deep breath and put as much distance between them as her office allowed. "We have to do this right, Caro. No more...of that. We can't give them anything else to fire back at us... you."

"They won't know," she countered, taking a step toward him. Dell backed all the way to the door, wrapping his hand around the solid knob. The cool metal helped ground him in what he needed to do.

"Yes, they will. They found out once, they'd find out again." At the stricken look on her face, he let go of the door and crossed to her. He kissed her, trying to convey all his anguish and love with the touch of his lips. She wiggled, trying to get closer to him, but he held her at a distance with his fingers clamped around her upper arms. She tasted like heaven, and he hated to let her go, but he had to. He broke the kiss, resting his forehead against hers. "Never doubt how much I want you, Caro, but we can't be together – not yet anyway. You need time to prove to them, and to yourself that you can do this." *And I do too.* "There's enough talk about you already, and I won't do anything to add to it." He pulled her close just to feel her in his arms one more time. "I hate what they said to you. It isn't right."

Those sweet hands found the skin at his back again and he held her tighter. None of this was right. They should be together. He should be able to tell her what was in his heart, but he couldn't, not until he'd earned the right to love her, and he had a damned long way to go before that happened, if ever.

"We'll get through this, and Hawkins Racing will be on top. I know it. I believe it."

"I want to believe it too, Dell. I really do."

"You do, Caro. You're the bravest person I know, taking on the established system like you have. I'm so sorry I made it harder for you."

She pushed away, and he reluctantly let her go. "Don't apologize, Dell," she said as she swiped the moisture from her cheeks with the back of her hand. "Please don't be sorry for...you know." She waved her hand in the air in an absent gesture. "I'm not."

His lips quirked up on one side and a little huff of purely masculine laughter escaped through them. "I'm not sorry about it

either, Caro. Never." His tone turned serious. "I am sorry someone
used what happened between us to hurt you. If I knew who did it, I'd
pay them a visit."

"I guess it's a good thing we don't know who it was, isn't it? My
driver is in enough trouble as it is; I can't have him suspended for
good." Her shaky little laugh eased his mind. She was going to be
okay. The spunky girl he knew was finding her way back.

"No, you can't, and I promise he'll be above reproach from now
on. I'm going to see to it myself."

☙❧

She believed him, even if it did make her all kinds of a fool for
doing so. He stood there with a big wet spot on his shirt from her
tears, acting all macho and protective, and so sure of himself. He
meant what he said. She just wasn't sure he would be able to follow
through. That bright young driver hadn't been seen in three years.
Was he still inside Dell? Or had the last three years buried him so
deeply Dell would never find him again?

And he was right about their relationship too. No matter how
much she wanted to be with him, to feel his arms around her, she
couldn't ignore the warnings. It wasn't right for her to be held to a
different set of standards than the men, but now wasn't the time to
take on that particular gorilla. One thing at a time, she vowed. First,
she needed to make Hawkins Racing a success. After that, she'd have
the clout to tackle the issue of equality. And if there was still
something between Dell and her then, she wasn't going to let it go.

Caro sent him on his way with a promise to compile a detailed
list of the company's debts, as well as an estimate of what it would
cost to be ready to race in two weeks. She hated to take Dell's money,
but he was right, she wasn't prepared to abandon her dream. If there
were even the slightest hope, she was going to grab at it with both
fists.

Chapter Fourteen

"You seriously need to work on your social skills," Warner said, taking the beer Dell offered and following him into the living room. "Do people actually come when you call them and say, 'Get over here,' and hang up?"

"You did, didn't you?" Dell waved his half-brother to his least favorite of the matching leather-covered recliners in the room. "What does that say about you?"

Warner took the indicated seat and settled in. "Point taken." He worked the lever on the side, raising the footrest. "I'm here. What do you want?"

"I don't know, exactly. I just thought we should talk."

"Feeling mortal, Dell? That was a nasty wreck."

"It makes a man think."

Silence stretched between them, broken only by the sound of aluminum popping as they drank. Dell finished his beer, or in this case, liquid courage. Staring straight ahead at the glossy black surface of his flat-screen TV, he said, "He knew about you."

Warner set his beer on the table between the two chairs. Dell didn't have to look to know Warner wasn't looking at him either.

"I don't have a middle name. Just the letter C. Richard C. Warner. You think that means anything?" Warner asked.

"I came first. Maybe your mother thought two kids named Caudell might be too obvious?" Dell said.

"Maybe," Warner said. "When I was a kid, I worshipped Caudell Wayne. Hell, I even had posters of him hanging in my room."

"And now?" Dell asked.

"I don't know. I hate how he died the way he did, and that I had anything to do with it, but I'd feel the same way no matter who it was."

"He worshipped you," Dell said. He felt Warner's gaze, but refused to look at the man. He continued, "He was always telling me what a good driver you were, and that I would never be as good as you. I hated you. But now it makes sense. He knew you were his son."

The statement hung in the air between them as they both digested what it meant.

"When I was a kid, Caudell was my hero, and I was jealous as all get-out that you were his son." Warner shook his head. "Man, I thought you had it all. We hung around the track a lot when I was a kid — Talladega. I grew up near there." He paused for another sip from his beer. "You and I started racing dirt tracks about the same time, I guess. I used to watch you and try to figure out how you did it. You always made it look so easy, where Caudell looked like every race was a struggle."

"You drive like him. And that's not a compliment," Dell said.

"I know," Warner said. "Believe me, I know."

"You look like him too," Dell said. "I never saw it before — probably because I wasn't looking for it, but the resemblance is there."

"You don't look anything like him," Warner said. "Except maybe the eyes. I only was around him a few times, but I'll never forget the way he could cut a person into little pieces with his eyes. You can do it too." Warner twirled his empty beer can between his thumb and forefinger. "Scary."

"No shit," Dell said, standing. "Want another beer?"

"Sure."

Dell returned with two cold ones. He handed one to Warner before resuming his seat.

"Sorry. I guess you probably know more about that look of his than anybody."

Dell swallowed, letting the cold liquid chill the anger building inside. He took another drink and reminded himself he'd invited Warner for this very reason — to talk about Caudell.

"Yeah. I think I still have a few scars from being sliced and diced by the old man. He always said I looked like my mother. I got the impression it was a reminder he'd rather not have in his face every day of the world."

"So, what happened to her?"

Dell shrugged. "I don't know. She left. I was little. End of story."

"Maybe she found out about me," Warner said.

Dell turned his head, scrutinizing his guest for the first time since he let him in the front door. "Maybe. Or one of the others."

"You think there are others?"

"It crossed my mind."

They both turned their attention to the drinks in their hands. Minutes ticked by, then Dell said, "She said she loves me."

"Who? Your mom?"

"No, you dickhead," Dell sighed. "Caro. She said it when I was kind of out of it – at the hospital. Or I might have dreamed it."

"And you're telling me this…why?"

"Haven't got a clue," Dell said, draining the rest of his beer. He got up, returning with two more. He handed one off to Warner. "Something's not right at Hawkins."

"Rumor is she's in over her head, management-wise, and financially."

"I'd buy the financial part, but the other? No way. She runs a tight ship, and she's smart."

"What are you going to do about it?"

"Don't know. A few weeks ago I wouldn't have cared. But now? Now I do. I'd like to see her make a go of it. She deserves a chance."

"Lots of people disagree with you. Renfro included."

"How did you end up driving for a bastard like him anyway?" Dell asked.

"I needed a ride. He offered. I never gave it much thought until the day Caudell died. This may sound weird, but when he told me Caudell was my dad, it was almost like he was amused that I was the one who caused the crash. I've turned it over in my head a million times and I can't make any sense of it. Everyone was crying, even the old-timers had tears in their eyes, but not Butch. I'd swear he was happy – delighted even, Caudell was dead."

Dell squinted at the blank TV screen as if it were a portal into the past. "I thought Butch and Caudell were friends, but now I think about it, they never did hang out together."

"I wouldn't read too much into it, Dell. Not many people like Butch Renfro, but he and Caudell had to have known each other pretty well. Hell, they raced against each other from the time they could both see over the top of a steering wheel."

Dell filed the information away to be examined some other time. Not that he gave a damn if Caudell had any friends, or enemies, for that matter. He changed the subject. "Why doesn't Renfro support Caro? Why would he care if she makes a go of it or not?"

Warner shrugged. "No idea. I assumed he was one of those men who think women don't have brains."

"Seems the racing world has a fair share of those," Dell said.

"Here's another funny thing," Warner said, leaning forward to rest his elbows on his knees. He held his beer can with both hands. "I can't say he took much of an interest in Hawkins Racing when she first took over. Everyone was talking about it. You know how it was. I'm sure there was plenty of talk around Anderson's garage too."

"Yeah, there was," Dell agreed.

"Anyway, Butch didn't have much to say on the subject – not until she took you on. After that he started coming in the garage, ranting about how she was an idiot, didn't have any business running a race shop...that sort of thing. It struck me as odd when he suddenly had an opinion, and not a nice one at that."

"You think it has something to do with me going to work for her?"

"Could be. He hates you."

"Really?" Dell asked. "Any idea why that is?"

"Not a clue," Warner answered. He stood. "Which way's the bathroom?"

Dell smiled. "Follow me," he said. "I've got something to show you."

"Can't it wait?" Warner asked as he fell in step behind Dell. "I gotta piss."

"Nope." Dell led Warner out the backdoor, across the patio and around the pool to where a wide swath of lawn stretched toward Lake Norman. He stopped in front of a wooden structure, too big to be a playhouse and too small to be a guesthouse. "Here we are," he said.

Warner took in the neat little building, then asked, "Okay, I give up. Where, exactly, are we?"

"Well," Dell said, pointing, "that's my dog house."

"I don't see any dogs," Warner said.

"I haven't gotten around to getting any yet."

"Is there a reason you're showing me this?" he asked, shifting uncomfortably in his need to relieve himself.

"Over there." Dell pointed to something glinting in the failing twilight.

"Is that a Darlington trophy?" Warner asked, moving to take a closer look.

"That's *the* Darlington trophy," Dell said.

Warner stopped in front of the impressive trophy, now a lawn ornament atop a low concrete platform. "The one you won... what's it doing out here?"

"It was either that or a fire hydrant. I thought this was more fitting." He unzipped and whipped out his dick. A yellow stream pinged against the gleaming silver trophy.

"Man, you got to get some dogs," Warner said, then he unzipped his pants.

❧

"I know I'm right." Caro stood toe-to-toe with Dell, refusing to back down. It was hell being this close to him and not touching him, but with the entire crew watching, all she could do was look her fill and pretend.

She might fool the crew, but she wasn't fooling Dell. She saw it in his eyes, in the set of his shoulders. He wanted her too. If she leaned in, he'd kiss her, and the professional distance they'd cultivated for the last two weeks would go up in smoke. And since they had no idea who told the AARA officials about their tryst a few weeks ago, it was imperative they maintain the charade in public. Caro vented her frustration on a sigh. "Look, Dell, just take the car out on the track one more time. If you don't see improvement, then we're done. I don't know what else we can do."

"I don't see how one adjustment is going to make a difference, Caro." He shook his head, two weeks of frustration showing on his face, and in his body language.

"I've run the calculations a dozen times. It's in the timing. There's no room for error with the new fuel injection system. You know that. This will do the trick. I'm sure of it."

"Yeah, yeah. I hear you." He slid into the driver's seat with the ease of experience. "One more time, Caro."

Banned from the circuit for the time being, they'd packed the hauler and headed west to South Carolina. The historic Greenville-Pickens track wasn't much to look at, but the half-mile oval was perfect for testing cars. No one would bother them, and the price was right – cheap. Caro missed the state-of-the-art equipment they'd left behind, but she had enough to work with. If she could find the power in the engine, they could fine tune as necessary when they got back to the Hawkins garage.

Dell took a few practice laps before he took the car up to its maximum speed on the short track. He'd know if the power were there, and if it were, they'd need to put her through the paces on a longer track – if not, they were back to square one. Caro crossed her fingers and her toes that she'd finally found the formula she was looking for.

"Looks good." Dell's voice held an element of enthusiasm she hadn't heard since they'd begun testing the new engine.

"How does she feel?" Caro asked.

"Like she could swallow the track whole," Dell said.

Caro blushed at his raw description. "Should we find her a longer track?" Caro asked.

"Hell, yes. I'm sorry I doubted you, Caro. She's purring like a whore suckin'…Ah, shit. She's running smooth, Caro. I can't wait to try her out on a longer track."

"Bring her in, Dell."

❈

They'd come so far in the last few weeks, and with a little luck and some help from the track fairies, they'd finally have a win. Just forty laps to go at Dover and Dell trailed the lead car by a car length.

"Lookin' good," Russell advised.

"I need fresh tires to catch him," Dell said.

"Hang tight. There's a lot of action in the pack. We'll pit under caution."

Dell held steady. If Russell were correct, the cars jockeying for position behind him would eventually get too aggressive and start knocking into each other. The caution flag would fly and all the leaders would pit for fuel and tires, maybe a last minute track-bar adjustment. He'd take the fuel and tires, but the car was handling good. He'd never driven a better car.

He had to hand it to Caro – the woman knew her cars. The mid-season suspension might have been the best thing that ever happened to Hawkins Racing. Caro made the adjustments she wanted, and had the time to test them out on an empty track. Dell smiled to himself. Caro was one hell of a woman, and he couldn't wait to celebrate today's win with her.

He was going to win. He had the power and track position to take the lead, but what was the point? Let Harbinger think he had it in the bag. His complacency would only make it easier for Dell to pass him in time to cross the finish line first.

Dell saw the track-side lights flash to yellow at the same time Caro's voice came over the headset. "Caution's out, Dell. Pit road is open."

"Comin' in. We have time for four," he said.

"Roger that, four tires," Russell acknowledged.

Dell maneuvered around the wreckage on the backstretch and slowed onto pit road right behind Harbinger. The pit crew did their job with swift efficiency, sending Dell out right where he wanted to be, on Harbinger's ass.

He lined up next to Harbinger for the restart. The pace car turned off the track and Dell hung back a fraction of a second, letting Harbinger jump out in front. He had plenty of time. No need to push it. The third place car made a bid for Dell's position, but with fresh tires and the faster car, Dell was beyond his reach. He dropped back. It was back to the status quo, just Dell and Harbinger, and soon, Dell thought, he'd take Harbinger out of the equation.

"Five laps," Jeff said from the spotter's roost atop the press box. "Clear all around."

Dell throttled up, closing the distance between his car and Harbinger's by a foot. He'd take one foot at a time, and before Harbinger realized it, he'd be in second place crossing the finish line. Dell eased up another foot.

"Shit," he said. "We've got trouble."

"What is it?" Russell asked.

"A shimmy in the right rear tire. Low air pressure?"

"Could be," Russell said. "How bad is it?"

Dell claimed another foot of track from Harbinger's lead. "It's not good. Fuck! What the hell happened? We've been running smooth all day."

"Can you keep her on the track?" Caro asked.

"I'm trying," Dell said. It was getting harder by the second. The rear end of the car was shaking like a can of spray paint in a tagger's hands. He backed off on the throttle and lost the few feet he'd gained on Harbinger.

"Two laps to go," Jeff said.

"Dell?" Caro questioned.

"I think I can hold onto second, but passing Harbinger is out of the question." Shit. What the hell happened? "I think we lost a lug," he said.

"White flag," Jeff said.

One more lap to the checkered. Dell made the decision. Missing lug or not, if he could hold onto the car, he might be able to nose past Harbinger in time to claim victory.

Dell throttled up. The wheel jerked beneath his hands, but he held on tight and eased up on Harbinger's ass, his car fighting him every inch of the way.

Move. Move. Move.

Finally, he got close enough to steal the lead car's air. Harbinger's rear end slid up the track.

"Clear," Jeff said.

Dell wrestled his car alongside Harbinger's. The rear tire shook hard enough to rattle his teeth but Dell refused to give up. A few feet more and he'd be in the lead. All he needed to do was be first across the line. An inch or a mile, it didn't matter. The money was the same either way.

His arms ached with the effort to keep the car on the track. Fuck. So close.

The finish line beckoned. Dell throttled up. The car shot forward, overtaking Harbinger by a nose, then all hell broke loose.

Dell fought the steering wheel as the backend of the car flew apart in a shower of sparks and a symphony of grinding metal.

"Fuck!"

"Dell!" Caro yelled in the headset.

Dell hung on, helpless, as the car spun and crossed the finish line, broken-ass first, half a car-length behind Harbinger.

The car came to a halt in the grass median. Dell lowered the window net and waved to let everyone know he was okay. He took his time unbuckling the safety harness.

"Carolina?"

"Dell? Are you okay?"

"Fine. Does second place count if you cross the line backwards?"

He heard her smile in her answer. "Yes, it does. Good work out there today."

"I'm sorry, Caro. I don't know what happened. I had the win."

"You'll get the next one, Dell."

He wasn't so sure. He'd done everything right today. For the first time since his father's death, he felt like it was the real Dell Wayne behind the wheel today. People thought he didn't notice his own driving. Hell, he wasn't blind. But until today, no matter how hard he tried, he couldn't seem to find his way back to the old Dell Wayne. He'd driven smart today – none of the aggressive shit he'd been living on for the last three years. The checkered flag should have been his.

Since his talk with Dickey Warner, he hadn't felt the restlessness he'd come to think was normal. He still didn't particularly like the guy, but they shared a bond that went beyond DNA. Caudell Wayne fucked up both their lives, and that was something they could bond over, even if they didn't know how to be brothers.

After their piss-fest on the Darlington trophy, they'd finished off the beers in Dell's refrigerator and gotten to know each other a little better. The alcohol loosened their tongues, and though Dell wouldn't go so far as to call Dickey his friend, he'd come to respect the guy. Dickey went from idolizing Caudell, to realizing he wasn't a god, to accidentally killing him, to finding out the man was his absentee father. In some ways, Dickey's life was more fucked up than Dell's, and that was saying something.

For Dell, having an ally in his hatred of his father made it easier. Caudell was gone, or he would be if Dell would loosen his grip and *let* him go.

Dell figured it was time to move on, put the past behind him. He didn't have a damned thing to prove to Caudell Wayne. The man made one son's life miserable, while he totally ignored the other. The past was the past. It was time to look to the future, and Carolina Hawkins was his future. She loved him. Granted, he might have imagined her saying those words, but he didn't care. If there was any chance she believed there was a man inside him worth loving, then he was going to find him – for her.

"Gotta go, Caro. My ride's here." Dell waved at the tow-truck driver.

Chapter Fifteen

Caro clenched the ladder rail with trembling hands as she climbed down from the war wagon into the nest of reporters waiting to talk to her. Dell ran a clean race today. Not a single accident until the end. Even then, he'd spun solo. Coming off his latest suspension, his dramatic second-place finish was big news. She pasted on a smile and turned to face the crowd.

A million questions later and she headed to the hauler. Finishing second meant post-race inspections, so they weren't going anywhere for a while. It was a nice problem to have, Caro mused. Maybe the inspection would turn up the problem with the rear wheel. Whatever it was, it happened after the last pit stop. A loose lug? It was the most likely answer. It wouldn't be the first time a tire changer failed to properly secure a lug. She made a mental note to remind both tire changers to practice as much as it takes to get the timing down, though they'd never had a problem before.

Still, Dell's life was on the line every time he took the car out of pit road, so there was no room for error on the part of the pit crew. Racing was dangerous enough without adding unnecessary risk.

Caro pulled a water bottle out of the small refrigerator and brought it to her lips, hating the way her hands still shook. Watching Dell spin out as he crossed the finish line nearly did her in. She curled up in the corner of the sofa and let her head fall back. It wasn't like she hadn't seen Dell wreck before, but after the last one that sent him to the hospital... well, it didn't bear thinking about.

She needed to get a grip on her emotions. She eyed the slight tremble on the surface of the water in the bottle she still held. This is what she got for loving a racecar driver, and now she understood why her father hadn't wanted this life for her. Would it ever get any easier? She didn't see how it could.

Her heart all but stopped when he reported the shimmy in the rear tire as her imagination went into overdrive conjuring up all kinds of horrible wrecks that might result from a tire failure at one hundred and sixty miles per hour. A shudder racked her body. She set the water bottle on the nearest table and wrapped her arms around her midsection.

The door opened, startling her. Caro jumped to her feet. Dell stood there, all in one piece. One delicious, sexy piece. She couldn't help it. She threw herself at him.

He caught her around the waist and held her tight. She splayed her hands over his back and pressed her cheek against his chest. His solid warmth banished the cold she hadn't been able to shake since he'd first mentioned the shimmy.

"It's okay, Caro."

"Let me hold you, Dell. Just for a minute."

They held each other, listening to the crew stowing everything in the back of the hauler not necessary for the post-race teardown.

"I thought…" Caro shuddered again. Dell stroked her back in long, lazy sweeps. "I was so scared."

"Shh," he soothed. "I know. I'm sorry. I don't know what happened."

"God, Dell. I don't know what I would do if anything happened to you."

Dell eased her away enough to place a finger beneath her chin and tilt her face up to his. They'd agreed to stay away from each other, but Caro couldn't care less about what anyone else thought of her. Right now, she needed the reassurance of Dell's kiss. Her lips parted in invitation.

"Nothing happened, Caro. I'm here. I'm fine." Then, to drive home his point, he kissed her.

All the anxiety of the last few laps fueled her need into a raging passion. She needed Dell. Needed to feel his skin beneath her hands – needed the solid evidence of him against her, inside her. She needed Dell like she needed her next breath. Nothing else mattered but having him close to her. And if the rest of the world disapproved, then to hell with them all.

"Dell," she said when they came up for air.

"I know we said we weren't going to do this, Carolina, but I need you."

Her heart sped up like a stuck throttle. She nodded in agreement. "I need you too, Dell. I don't care what they say."

"I do, Caro. I care – a lot." His words put distance between them, but he didn't move.

Please don't say no. She opened her mouth to protest. His hips ground against hers and the shaft of his desire dug into her belly. The words died on her lips. Her heart raced with the knowledge that he wanted her as much as she wanted him.

"I wanted to wait until the season was over, or at least until you proved your point to the old boys' club, but I can't, Caro. I need you too much. You're all I think about, day and night. And God almighty," he ran his hand down to cup her ass, "this fire suit makes me insane."

She smiled at the gravel in his voice. "I could say the same about you," she said. "I don't know what it is about it, but I want to rip it off you every time I see you in it."

He cupped her face in his palm. His thumb brushed her lips in a tender caress. His eyes reflected his own wicked smile. "I'll wear it for you later, someplace private."

"Promise?" she asked.

"Promise," he said.

He kissed her again. This time, the banked passion simmered below the surface like a trophy awaiting the winner. Caro trembled again, but it had nothing to do with being cold and everything to do with the man whose lips heated her blood and stirred her soul.

❧

Dell couldn't wait to have Caro in his arms again. She'd been more than willing back at the track, but they'd agreed on discretion. The wait made the prize that much more special. She offered her hand, and he led her through the lobby to the bank of elevators. They waited in silence and rode to the upper floor, letting their hands speak for them as they met, palm-to-palm, fingers intertwined.

He'd chosen this hotel in a small town off the usual route between Dover and Charlotte. No one would know them here, but still, he wouldn't jump her in the elevator, even though he wanted to. Tonight, Carolina would be his – the old boys' club be damned.

"I hate having to sneak around," he said, pulling her into his arms as soon as the room door clicked shut behind them, sealing the rest of the world out.

"I'm through worrying about what they say about me," Caro said.

"I'm not," Dell said. "I hate sneaking, but I'd hate the gossip more. I won't give them any more ammunition to use against you, Carolina." He cupped her face between his palms. "You mean too much to me. I want to see you succeed, and I'll do anything I can to help you, and that includes making sure I don't do anything to make it harder for you." He kissed her, long and slow, infusing the kiss with everything he felt for her and couldn't put into words.

"Well, I sure hope you make something hard for me," she said with a twinkle in her eye.

"Oh, God, Carolina," he laughed and pulled her against his erection. "You never have to worry about that. Do you have any idea how difficult it is to race with a hard-on?"

Her hand closed over the hard length of him through his jeans, making him groan.

"You've got on too many clothes," she said as her fingers found the top button and began to work it free. It seemed to take forever, and then she went to work on the next one. He took over, silently vowing to invest in some jeans with zippers for expediency. God, he wanted to feel her small hands on him – everywhere – almost as much as he wanted to touch her.

He worked the final button free, and in one motion, shoved his jeans and briefs to his knees. His cock sprang free like a thoroughbred out of the chute. Caro wrapped her hand around him and his knees almost buckled. "Shit, Carolina. That feels so good."

She wiggled her other hand underneath his shirt. He watched it bunch around her wrist as her hand slid over his stomach to his chest. A none-to-gentle push pinned his shoulders against the door. The top of her head sank lower, and lower. His little brain was in charge of his body now, so he didn't realize her intent until his dick disappeared, slipping between her lips, the last remaining inches clamped tight in her fist while the fingers of her other hand found his ass.

He couldn't look away. What was left of his scrambled brain screamed at him to make her stop. He fisted his fingers in her hair and willed them to force her away, but with each lick, each suck of her soft, sweet tongue, he lost another million brain cells. So instead of making her stop, he held on for dear life and let her have her way with his dick.

Thank God for the door. Every time his cock slid past her lips he moved a step closer to death. But, heaven help him, he wanted to go this way. The only thing better would be dying with his cock buried deep inside her pussy. The thought gave him the strength to push her face out of reach of his cock. "Carolina. I've got to have you. Now."

Her gaze lifted to his. She ran her tongue over her swollen pink lips and he almost shoved his cock past them again. The look she gave him told him she wouldn't mind, but hell, he minded. Her mouth was sweet as hell, but his body remembered another sweeter spot and he was going to have it – now.

"You taste good," she licked her lips again.

"Good God, woman." He lifted her by her armpits and dragged her body against his. He crushed his mouth against hers, tasted himself on her lips and groaned. "I've never wanted anything or anyone as much as I want you, Carolina Hawkins."

She reached between them and clamped her hand around his aching dick. "I want you too, Dell." She tugged once, twice and he closed his eyes to concentrate on breathing. "Make love to me."

He sucked in a ragged breath as she released him and stepped back. Piece by piece, her clothes dropped to the floor at his feet until she stood naked before him – a masterpiece of soft female perfection. He reached a hand out to touch her and she took a step back. He tried to follow and nearly face-planted on the carpet as the jeans around his knees brought him up short.

She laughed – a wicked, seductive laugh. "You're wearing too many clothes, Dell."

❧

He growled like a wild animal trapped and taunted. He grabbed a condom from his pocket and clamped the packet in his teeth as he fought his way out of his clothes. He'd never undressed so fast in his life. He ripped the packet open and sheathed himself, then he stalked her to the bed. It didn't matter his prey made no attempt to escape. She'd ignited something uncivilized inside him, something that clawed to get out.

Her legs bumped against the mattress and he closed the distance between them. He stood over her, drinking in her scent and the heat radiating off her body. She tilted her face up. Her gaze locked with his and there was no mistaking the look in her eyes. She wanted him as much as he wanted her.

He lifted a hand to the back of her head and grabbed a fistful of her hair in a hard grip. She gasped, but made no attempt to stop him when he jerked her forward. Her hard nipples speared his chest.

His other hand came up to cradle her jaw. He stroked his thumb over the corner of her lips. He tugged her mouth open and slipped his thumb inside, dragging her mouth roughly to the side. She swirled her tongue around the digit and he groaned at the erotic enticement. "I don't want to be gentle, Caro. I need you too much." She nodded her understanding. His hand moved to her ass, squeezing and kneading. "I won't hurt you."

"I know, Dell. I know."

He searched her eyes for any trace of fear and saw only a hunger and desperation equal to his own.

"Mine," he said. Then his lips were on hers. A moment later, she was under him, opening for him. He took her, fast and hard. She wrapped her legs around his hips and matched him thrust for thrust. His lips and hands explored, as did hers.

There was nothing gentle about the way they took from each other, but they gave in equal measure, and when Caro came, she took Dell with her into a world where there was no wrong, no censorship, no condemnation, only right. She led him through the darkness and showed him the light. He looked in her eyes and saw the thing he feared most in life, her love. He'd never be worthy of it, but buried inside her, his cock bathed in it, he was certain it was the only thing he'd ever need. He'd spent too many years trying to earn the love of a man who could never give it when he was alive, and sure wasn't going to give it from the grave.

None of it mattered now. Only Carolina mattered, and he'd do anything to earn the love he saw in her eyes.

"Carolina. My sweet, Carolina," he whispered into the crook of her neck. Her arms encircled his shoulders as he poured himself inside her one wretched spasm at a time.

Caro held Dell in her arms as his cock jerked inside her. His hips pumped, grinding against her in the same jerky rhythm. She should be shocked at the way they'd come together, like two animals in heat. The only thing missing were the teeth and claws, and she couldn't be too sure about those.

Spent, Dell collapsed on top of her, instantly rolling to the side and dragging her with him.

"Jesus, Caro. I'm sorry."

Beneath her palm, Dell's heart thumped a wild beat. "Don't be. I'm not."

One roughened hand stroked the small of her back. "I should have taken more care. I wasn't thinking of your pleasure, only mine. I'm sorry."

"Stop it, Dell," she said. "I'm fine. Well, mostly fine." She inched her hand across his chest to trace the flat disk around his nipple. He hissed and tightened his hold on her. "Not that it wasn't satisfying, it was. But it was awfully...quick."

"Are you saying I crossed the finish line too fast?"

She continued to tease his nipple as she spoke. "No, what I'm saying is it was a short race. Maybe next time, instead of a drag race, we could try a Le Mans."

"Some of those races go on for twenty-four hours," Dell pointed out.

Caro raised up on an elbow and smiled. "I know."

⋘⋙

He couldn't exactly call it a habit, but he and Warner spent their last few days off together, mostly drinking beer and watching old movies at Dell's house. Warner said his apartment was too small for two people, though why he hadn't bought himself a house was beyond Dell's comprehension. As long as he kept showing up with cold beer, Dell didn't care.

"I hope you didn't bring the same shit you did last week," Dell said as Warner headed to the kitchen with the requisite brown bag.

"You didn't have to drink it."

Dell held out his hand. "Just give me one, and shut up."

Warner handed Dell a bottle and took one for himself before they headed to the recliners in the living room. "Talladega's coming up," he said.

"So it is," Dell said, popping the top on his brew and taking a long pull. "What about it?"

"If you need a drafting partner, I might be interested."

Dell studied his half-brother. "What would Renfro think?"

"I don't give a shit what he thinks. He's been talking a lot of trash around the shop the last few weeks, and I don't like it."

"What kind of trash?"

"Stuff. He's coming down real hard on Caro Hawkins and you, too. You'd think he'd be mindful of who he's talking about, since he knows about our relationship, but he doesn't know we talk, so I guess he thinks it's all right to talk shit about you in front of me."

"So, you want to get back at him by drafting with me?"

"Maybe. It would serve him right if I pushed you across the finish line in first place."

Dell grinned. "Yeah, that would be poetic, but what makes you think it wouldn't be you crossing first with me biting your ass?"

"Because I don't want to win? Renfro is being a real asshole. If I win, so does Renfro Racing, and right now, I'm not in a frame of mind where that seems right. I'd much rather see Hawkins Racing get the trophy."

"No offense, but I would too. Okay. But I have to tell Caro before the race. I don't want her blowing a gasket if you suddenly start kissing my ass around the track."

"Drafting, Dell. Don't flatter yourself. I won't be kissing your ass, on the track or off. I'll leave that for the pretty lady you're seeing."

Chapter Sixteen

Caro couldn't remember a time in her life when she'd felt this good. For the last three weeks, she and Dell had stolen as many minutes to be together as possible without drawing attention to their intimate relationship. They had yet to work in a Le Mans, but every encounter wasn't a drag race either. Her body hummed with satisfaction, and love for Dell.

So far, he'd lived up to the promise he made when they struck their financial agreement. He no longer drove every race as if he had a death wish. The brilliant race strategist was back, but he'd yet to win a race.

Caro was beginning to think Hawkins Racing was jinxed. There'd been the issue with the loose lug nut that cost Dell a win, and might have resulted in a serious wreck. Thankfully, no one was injured in the spinout. Even the car survived. She still cringed when she thought about the findings from the post-race inspection. The offending lug nut looked as if someone had filed down the threads on the inside. It was unclear if the damage occurred on the track or if the lug was damaged when it was put on during Dell's final pit stop. Caro questioned the tire carrier – the guy who glued the lugs to the wheels before each race, and he swore he checked each lug before it went on the wheel.

She kept the lug in her desk drawer as a reminder something as small as a lug could end a successful run.

But the lug episode was only the first of a series of bizarre incidents that occurred over the last three races. None of them were serious, but every one of them cost Dell valuable track position. Caro gave credit where it was due. Dell kept a calm head through it all. She wished she could say the same for herself. Frustration gnawed at her. The car was running like nothing else on the track. Dell was out-driving every other driver on the track, but they still hadn't brought home a single trophy.

Caro left the garage at Talladega, heading to her motor coach for a much-needed nap before qualifying. She wouldn't trade her stolen nights with Dell for anything, but she found, on occasion, she needed to make up for the lost sleep. This was one of those times. Between spending time with Dell and making adjustments on the car for the longer Superspeedway at Talladega, she'd had little time to herself.

She wound her way through the maze of giant motor homes, her attention focused on the changes they'd made this morning. Not only did they have to adjust for the longer track, but the Alabama weather wasn't helping either. The track temperature during practice runs earlier in the week were below normal, but for qualifying, the weatherman predicted record high temperatures. Everything they'd done needed to be rethought and recalculated, the adjustments made. And, to top it off, it was possible the weather would change yet again before the race began tomorrow.

Caro was lost in her thoughts so she didn't notice the man leaning against the motor coach parked next to hers until it was too late. She jumped when he spoke.

"Hello, Carolina."

"Oh, Butch! You scared me."

"Sorry." He pushed away from the coach and joined Caro at the door to her motor home. "I wanted to have a word with you."

She couldn't think of a single person she wanted to talk to less than she did Butch Renfro. Opening the door, she stepped inside and Butch followed, closing the door behind him. Fatigue weighed on her shoulders and her patience. She crossed her arms over her chest and leaned against the small kitchen counter. "What do you want?" she asked.

"How much longer are you going to keep this up, Carolina? You're dragging this out longer than is necessary, and your stubbornness is only going to make it harder on your employees when you finally do go under. No one else is going to take them on this late in the season."

"I don't need you to tell me that, Butch. Things are turning around for Hawkins Racing. My employees aren't going to be looking for new jobs in the middle of the season, or when the season is over." At least she prayed it was true. If Hawkins Racing went under, she'd be looking for a job with another team herself, and paying Dell's investment back for the rest of her life.

"You're stubborn and delusional. It seems your screw-up of a driver finally got his shit together, but he still hasn't won a race. Your team is incompetent, from the engineers all the way down to the lowliest member of the pit crew."

Caro bristled at the blatant insult to her team. "You don't know anything about my team, and they aren't responsible for the things that happened. Lug nuts fail. The split O-ring on the hydraulic jack was a fluke, and it's certainly not their fault the supplier screwed up and didn't deliver fresh gas cans to our pit on time. Shit happens, Butch. We've just experienced more than our share lately."

"Yeah, and from what I hear, you're having more than your share of that shit driver of yours too." Caro froze. She watched in mute horror as Butch closed the distance between them. Her skin crawled at the way he looked at her, as if he... no, it was too disgusting to think. Before she could dodge him, he pressed himself up against her. The fingers of one hand dug into her hip, the other clasped the back of her head, anchoring her against him. His erection pressed into her stomach. She opened her mouth to scream, but he silenced her with a kiss that made her stomach lurch. Bile rose in her throat and she fought back with everything she had. She pushed, she kicked, she tried to bite him. He fisted his hand in her hair and held her tighter.

When he finally came up for air, Caro turned and vomited in the sink. Behind her, Butch Renfro laughed. "My money is as good as Dell Wayne's, little girl. When he gets tired of paying to get inside your fire suit, come see me. I might take his place, but you'll have to offer me more than he's getting. I want it all, Caro, and if I have to fuck you to get it, I will." He moved to the door, stopping before he opened it and threw his parting words at her with a leering smile. "I still know how to show a woman a good time, especially one with such low standards."

Caro made it to the door, threw the lock, and wobbled back to the sofa. She curled up in a ball, wrapping her arms around her knees to stop the shaking. She'd never been so disgusted in her life. Butch

Renfro was old enough to be her father! And he knew about her and Dell. It was impossible for him, or anyone else to know. She and Dell never said more than was necessary to each other around the garage, or at the track. As far as the racing world was concerned, their relationship was a professional one. Renfro couldn't know. He had to be guessing, but that didn't make what he'd done any less sickening.

She sat for the longest time, wondering what, if anything she could do about Renfro's assault, ultimately deciding there wasn't a thing she could do. Even if she did go to the track officials, who would believe her? There were no witnesses, and if she accused Renfro of sexually assaulting her he'd no doubt drag out proof of her illicit relationship with her driver. He'd turn it all back on her. Who'd believe a slut like her? Any woman who'd whore herself out to fund her race team wouldn't stop at sleeping with one sugar daddy. Renfro would have them all believing she'd come to him, and propositioned him instead of the other way around.

The whole thing made her sick to her stomach. She called Russell and told him the heat was too much for her, and she'd watch qualifying from her motor home instead of the war wagon. He didn't question her, and Caro showered until the hot water tank ran out, then curled up on the bed to think.

Renfro's words kept coming back to her. She didn't believe for a second he wanted her. He wanted Hawkins Racing. But why? Why not expand his own shop? Money wasn't an issue. It didn't make any sense. No one else was beating down her door, or sexually assaulting her, to coerce her into selling.

When Dell called her after qualifying, she congratulated him on his fourth place starting slot and declined his offer to meet her in the hauler later for a quickie.

"We agreed to keep our relationship away from the track," she said. No way would she tell Dell about Renfro's visit, or that all their discretion had been for naught. Renfro had found out. And if they broke their own rule and hooked up at the track, others would figure it out too.

"I know, Caro. I have something I want to tell you. It's part personal, and part business. Can't we meet somewhere?"

"Not tonight, Dell, if you don't mind. This heat is getting to me today. I just want to lay in the air conditioning and rest. Besides, I need to go over the EFI settings again. This new electronic fuel injection system takes more time than a carburetor, if you can believe that."

Dell chuckled. "Thrown over for a fuel injection system. I never thought I'd hear a woman use that excuse for staying away from me."

"It's not an excuse," she lied. "I really do need to make sure we have the optimal settings for the race."

"You never rest, do you, Caro? Okay, what I have to say can wait. I'll see you tomorrow."

"Thanks, Dell. Have fun tonight at the Nationwide Series race." She'd originally planned to sit in the stands with her team and watch the lower division race, but she wasn't ready to see Dell, or anybody, after what had happened with Renfro. She needed more time to think, and to erase the memory of his touch from her lips and her skin. When she was with Dell again, she didn't want any part of the episode to come between them.

That evening, she dissected every word Renfro said. Had she sold herself to Dell for funding? No. She didn't feel she had, and she was certain Dell didn't either. Renfro dropped the poisoned idea in her head just to mess with her. She couldn't let it get to her. She loved Dell, and though he hadn't said the words, she was certain he loved her too. Their relationship had nothing to do with the money.

She was more prepared to see Dell the following day, having convinced herself Renfro's words were meant to mess with her head, with no basis in truth. She noticed Dell first, standing to one side, talking to a reporter. She returned his subtle wave.

Caro went through her usual pre-race routine, checking to see everything was in order, paying closer attention to the little things, like hydraulic jacks and lug nuts.

She checked, and rechecked everything. Caro stood by as they rolled the car out for the final inspection, confident the car was in perfect order. Hawkins Racing needed to win at Talladega. The monster 2.66-mile Superspeedway was the perfect setting to show off the new Hawkins Racing engine Caro worked so hard on for the last few years in anticipation of the time when AARA would scrap the old carburetor system for the more fuel-efficient electronic fuel injectors.

She was looking over the latest computer readout from the Engine Control Unit when Dell approached. He wasn't alone.

"Carolina," he said. "Do you remember Dickey Warner?"

The man beside Dell extended his hand. Caro placed her hand in his for a short, but polite handshake. She turned her gaze to Dell, silently questioning why he'd bring Butch Renfro's best driver to her garage – before the biggest race yet for their team.

Dell addressed Richard. "Can you give us a minute?" he asked.

Warner ambled outside and pretended an interest in the flagpole visible on top of the press box. "Why did you bring him here?" she asked, aware of the accusation in her voice.

"Whoa, Caro. I don't know what you're thinking, but I assure you, it's wrong. Just let me tell you, then you can ask all the questions you want."

"Fine," she huffed. "Tell me."

Dell ran one hand through his hair in a nervous gesture. Well, he should be nervous, bringing Warner around. He glanced at Warner standing just outside hearing range, signing autographs for a few hot-pass fans. He turned to her. "He's my brother."

"What?" she screeched.

"It's true," Dell said.

Caro grabbed him by the sleeve of his fire suit and dragged him deeper into the shop. "What the hell are you saying?"

"I'm saying, Richard Warner is my brother. Half-brother, at least. He's a bastard."

"Of course he's a bastard, Dell. He's the one who pushed your dad into the wall, and he's tried to kill you a time or two I recall as well."

"Yeah, well… he says it was an accident. That he didn't know Caudell was his dad until after the crash. Renfro told him."

"And he believed him?"

"Not at first, but his mother confirmed it."

Caro looked around Dell to see the man outside. Now that she thought about it, he did look a little like Caudell, Senior. Not so much like Dell, but Dell took after his mother, or so Caro believed. She'd never met the woman. "So, why did you bring him here? Today?"

"He says he's sorry about what happened to Caudell, and after the way Renfro blurted out the daddy news, Dickey says there's no love lost between the two of them. Anyway, he's offered to draft with me today."

"Are you fuckin' out of your mind?" Caro hissed the words through clenched teeth. "No. No. And, no."

"Caro – "

"I said, no, Dell. You can win without a drafting partner. Besides, with the new rear bumpers, it's not as easy as it once was. One mistake from *Dickhead*, and you'll be nose into the wall. Have you forgotten Daytona? That was less than two months ago."

"I haven't forgotten, but that was then. If he wanted to take me out of the race, he wouldn't offer to draft with me, he'd just shove me into the wall and keep going. He doesn't need my permission to kill me." Dell fisted his hands on his hips. "Look, Caro. You'll just have to trust me on this. We know the risk. We won't draft unless I need the extra speed to win. I know you have the fuel injector thing down, and we have the fastest car on the track. I purposely held some back in qualifying so no one would know what we've got under the hood. But this is insurance, Caro. Just in case."

"The only kind of insurance anyone from Renfro is offering is disaster insurance, Dell. This is guaranteed to be a disaster."

"I don't think so, Caro. I've hated the guy since I first laid eyes on him when we were kids, but he seems sincere. I trust him. He wants to leave Renfro. If you get Hawkins Racing in the black, maybe we could take him on next year. Field two Cup cars instead of one. I'd like to see Hawkins as successful as it once was."

Dell had grown two heads, or maybe she was seeing double in her rage. "Don't do anymore thinking for me, Dell. Just drive the fucking car, and do it without *Dickhead* or anyone else associated with Renfro. I won't stand for it."

Dell squared his shoulders. Even the air seemed to stand still as he stared down at her. "Well, Ms. Hawkins. I don't give a good goddamned what you will or won't stand for. I've got money at stake here too, and if I can use Dickey to win this race, by God, that's what I'm going to do."

Dell left without a backward glance, collected his new buddy and headed in the direction of the track. Echoes of Butch Renfro's words rang in her ears. Maybe Dell was after more than what was in her fire suit. Maybe he was using her body to get what he really wanted, her company. Maybe he was conspiring with Renfro. It didn't seem likely, but nothing that happened since she took over Hawkins Racing seemed likely.

She pasted on a smile for the cameras and joined in the pre-race festivities, all the while her heart was breaking, and her confidence waning. How could she have fallen for Dell? Somehow, he convinced her he was the one person in the business who believed she had every right to be a team owner. She'd bought into his act too. He was no better than Renfro – maybe even worse. At least Renfro was straight up about his intentions – offering to buy her out, and when that didn't work, offering to fuck her to get what he wanted.

Dell had gone about it in a more underhanded way. He seduced his way into her heart and her bed, made her believe in him – then he snuck his way into her company. She'd given him her heart and believed his financial backing was given out of friendship and his genuine belief in her. And all the time, she'd done exactly what Butch Renfro accused her of. She'd sold her body for money. Dell's money. And in the process, she'd lost control of Hawkins Racing.

Dell and Dickhead would do whatever they wanted, and there wasn't a damn thing she could do to stop them.

Caro almost forgot about her misery as the race progressed. Dell held track position throughout the race, seemingly without effort. He stayed out of every crash and skirted disaster with a steady hand on the wheel. While others tried drafting with various levels of success, Dell cruised into second place early and hung on.

He'd have to pit again for tires and fuel, but barring any unseen accidents, Dell could make a serious bid for the lead, and ultimately, the win in the last few laps. Everything he did looked like it was scripted. A few drivers made serious bids for his position, but he'd cut them off with skill and finesse.

"The temperature dropped," Caro advised. "You should see a drop in engine temperature soon. Open her up when you think the time is right – she'll give you all the power you need."

"I can feel it, Caro. Damn, this car is responsive – kind of reminds me of someone," Dell said.

"Shut up and drive, Dell," Caro warned.

Caro kept a close watch on Warner. He'd run fourth for most of the race, and in a few instances it appeared he might actually be protecting Dell's back. She shook her head to dislodge the ridiculous notion. If Warner was sticking close to Dell, it had to be so he could make sure Dell didn't win. No way would she believe Warner had Dell's best interest in his heart, fully apologetic half-brother or not. It didn't compute with what she knew.

"Pit with everyone else, Dell," Caro said. "All the leaders are coming in under the green flag for tires and fuel."

"Ten-four. Coming in," he said.

Twenty laps to go. Dell and the other top ten leaders made it to their pits and back out in record time. A few lost track position due to poor performances from their pit crews, but not Dell or any of the top four.

"Thanks, guys. Great job," he praised the crew, then opened up his lead.

"No one can catch you, Dell," Caro said.

"Roger that. No drafting today. I'm on my own."

She couldn't contain her excitement, despite her earlier dark thoughts. Dell was going to win this one, and he was going to do it without any help from Warner, or Renfro, or anyone else. All the work she'd done on the engine, on the fuel injection system was finally going to pay off. Victory was theirs. She felt it in her bones.

"Bring it home, Dell."

"This one's for you, Caro."

Chapter Seventeen

It felt fucking great to be back in Victory Lane. Dell smiled for the cameras and splashed champagne on everyone – Caro included. He didn't have a clue what had been going on in her head before the race, but she was smiling now. It was ridiculous, but he was glad he had a part in putting the smile on her face, and he planned on putting a different kind of smile there as soon as he could get them both away from this media frenzy.

Her engine was amazing. Even before the cold front moved in and the temperature dropped, he sensed she had it in her to win. He'd never driven a smoother ride, or one with the kind of power this one had. If Caro were able to duplicate the results, she'd set the racing world on its ear, and he'd have all his goddamned money back in no time.

He pushed thoughts of Caudell's money out of his head. He'd figure out some way to get rid of it, but he didn't have to be in a hurry. At least it served some purpose, helping Caro get over the rough spot and on the downhill slide to true success. He caught a glimpse of her out of the corner of his eye. Her ponytail had fallen down and her champagne-soaked hair was plastered to her head. Her face glowed with vitality and victory as she answered a reporter's questions. Soon, the whole world would know about the female team owner who also designed and helped build the engine of the future.

And she was his.

Someone dumped more champagne on his head and he turned to return the favor. Caro was his. He could share her for these few minutes knowing he'd be the one to peel her wet clothes off her body tonight. He imagined the way her skin would taste, the distinct flavor of Carolina with a hint of champagne.

"Hey, Trent," he called to one of the pit crew. "Grab one of those champagne bottles and stash it in my locker in the hauler." Trent hustled off to do Dell's bidding.

Dell accepted macho man-hugs and gave as many champagne showers as he got, all the while planning his own private celebration later. When he'd have Caro all to himself.

&

Dell moved aside as the crew pushed the car to the garage under the watchful eyes of the track officials. The teardown and inspection would take several hours – hours Dell intended to spend naked with Carolina. He scanned the thinning crowd, but she was nowhere to be seen. His gaze landed on the lone figure standing near the fence.

"Dickey," Dell said, extending his hand. Their palms connected in a civilized handshake.

"Dell. Congratulations."

"Thanks. And thanks for the help. I didn't see it, but I hear you blocked Johnson from making a run at me near the end."

Warner shrugged. "He wasn't going to take the lead, but he might have caused all kinds of havoc trying."

"Well, thanks anyway. I appreciate it, and I'm sure Caro does too." He scanned the area again. Still no sight of her petite frame among the remaining celebrators.

"I've got to go," Warner said. "I wanted to offer my congratulations. You didn't need my help today, and with the new engine, I doubt you will ever again, but just in case…"

"I appreciate it, Dickey. I really do."

Warner nodded. "Okay then. I'll be going now." He took a few steps and turned back. "Look, Dell. I'm not going to pretend we're friends, but if you need anything, anything at all, just shout."

He didn't wait for a reply. Dell watched Warner's retreating back until someone laid a hand on his shoulder, commanding his attention for yet another interview.

It was later than he expected when he finally returned to his motor coach. He showered quickly, anxious to find Caro for the private celebration he'd been mentally planning ever since he crossed the finish line. He made some adjustments to the plan. By now, she would have changed out of her champagne-soaked fire suit, and that was a damn shame.

He was fishing for his shoes under the bed when his cell phone rang. He grabbed it off the bed with one hand while the other snagged one wayward shoe.

"Hey, Russell."

"Dell. Can you come down to the garage?"

Dell fished the other shoe out and sat on the end of the bed to put them on. "I've got plans, Russell. Can we save the celebration until we get home?"

"Trust me, Dell. You wanna be here for this. Now get your ass down here. Now."

Russell's clipped tone sent a cold spear of dread through Dell's body. "Okay. I'm putting my shoes on. I'll be there in a few minutes."

He tried calling Caro, but the call went immediately to voicemail. This couldn't be good. It wasn't unusual for little things to come up in a post-race inspection, but he couldn't imagine what it might be. The car met all the specifications to the letter. Caro was too meticulous for it to be anything but perfect. And she was too smart to think she would get away with cheating.

His feet felt like he'd put on concrete shoes instead of his favorite running shoes. He kept his head bent, avoiding eye contact with the people he met on the way. It surprised him how many people were still hanging around. Most of them were fans who were probably planning an early start with their motor homes in the morning instead of fighting the crowds clogging the roads tonight.

The lights blazed in the garage. All work had stopped and about a dozen people stood around talking in small clusters. Dell recognized the Hawkins crewmembers and a few people from AARA. The men in the white fire suits were the observers, there to keep an eye on everyone and everything. His gaze stopped on Caro. She stood off to one side, dwarfed by the cluster of men around her. None of them looked happy, especially Caro.

"Hey," Dell said, approaching the group. "What's going on?"

A flash of relief crossed her face as she looked up at him, but she masked it so fast Dell wasn't sure he'd seen it at all. He shook hands with a few of the men who offered. He recognized most of them. These were the men who enforced the rules, the ones who seemed to delight in suspending him at every turn. The cold spear of dread he felt earlier turned to a block of ice in his gut.

"I'm glad you're here," Caro said. "It seems we have a problem."

Dell ignored the officials, locking his gaze on Caro. She was trying to be strong, but the stress was taking a toll on her. Her shoulders slumped and dark circles rimmed her beautiful eyes. He wanted to take her in his arms and hold her until he could make all the bad things in her life go away. "What kind of problem? It can't be with the engine. She's special, but well within the specifications," he said.

"Not the engine – the fuel."

Dell glanced around the group of somber faces. "What about the fuel?"

"The post-race tests show an illegal performance-enhancing additive," this from the guy with *Stan* stitched over the pocket of his white AARA shirt.

"How did it get there?" Dell asked.

Silence. Half a dozen pairs of eyes turned to him. Dell held up his hands.

"Whoa. You don't think I had anything to do with it." This was unreal. From the looks on their faces, it was exactly what they were thinking. He ignored them and looked at Caro.

"Not you too. Caro. Seriously?"

More silence.

"Fuck!" Dell turned and walked away, stopping when he got to the car. He tried to process the information. Of course the officials would think he'd done it, but Caro? Her lack of faith cut him to the core. He rubbed the back of his neck and tried to think. How could this happen? Who could have done it, and why?

Well, the why was easy enough. He could think of only two reasons to use an additive. Either someone wanted to give the car an edge, or someone thought he had a chance of winning and wanted to make sure the car got disqualified if it did.

Everyone in their garage believed the car was good enough to win. None of them would use an additive to give them an edge. That left the other reason, and Dell didn't have to look far to find a host of people who would want his car disqualified.

Someone touched his arm. He recognized her touch. Caro.

"Dell," she said.

"I didn't do it, Caro. I can't believe you would think I would do something so stupid."

"They searched the hauler. The empty can was in your locker."

"You're shittin' me, right? Do I look stupid, Caro? And when was I supposed to have done this? While I was circling the track at one hundred and ninety miles per hour? Or maybe I hopped out during one of the thirteen-second pit stops, ran to the hauler, grabbed some fuckin' additive, ran back to the pit, somehow managed to get it into the tank without anyone seeing and ran back to the hauler to stash the empty can in my locker where anyone could find it, and still get back in the car and out on the track. Yeah, I'm guilty."

"I don't think you did it, Dell. I know you didn't. But someone did."

"Well, it damn sure wasn't me."

"The car is disqualified and they're talking about taking the win away as a penalty."

Dell raised his face to the ceiling and counted to ten. This couldn't fuckin' be happening.

"I think I know who did it, or at least who's behind it."

Dell snapped his head down. "Yeah, I have a pretty good idea myself. But how did he do it? He has to have someone in our garage or the pit crew."

"Or maybe someone who has access to the gas cans before they get to the pits."

Dell ran it through his head. "No. There's no way of knowing which cans are going to which pits until they get there. It had to be done after the can was delivered to our pit stall."

Caro nodded. "You're right. And anyone could have put the empty container in your locker. The hauler is open, and there aren't any locks on the lockers."

"That narrows it down, at least."

"I can't believe one of our own could do this to us," Caro said, scanning the clusters of men standing around waiting for instructions. "Maybe they thought they were helping."

"I thought about that too, but they all believed we had a winning car. They're all behind you, one hundred percent, Caro. I talked to them a few weeks ago. None of them would have done this. The only reason to do it was so this would happen." Dell waved his hand to indicate the fiasco around them. "Someone wanted the car disqualified, and you and I both know who it is."

"Yes, we do. I never thought he'd go this far. I thought he was more into personal intimidation."

"What are you talking about? Personal intimidation? Did he do something else you haven't told me about?" He'd kill the fucker if he laid a hand on Caro.

"I wasn't going to tell you, but tonight pushes the bounds of fair play. Renfro has gone too far this time."

Dell listened as Caro related the incident in her motor home. The block of ice in his gut turned to cold, hard steel, sharp enough to cut anyone in his way into tiny pieces. And Butch Renfro was in his way.

"I'm going to kill him."

"No! Dell!" Caro ran after him.

"You can't stop me, Caro," he yelled over his shoulder. "The bastard had no right to touch you."

Caro caught up to him and stopped him by yanking on his arm. He stopped long enough to dislodge her fingers from his sleeve. "Wait, Dell. Let's do this the right way. I'll tell the officials what happened. They'll believe me now. They'll handle Butch."

"You're mine, Carolina. No one touches you. No one *assaults* you and gets away with it."

"Dell, you have to stop. I know you want to beat up on Butch, but it won't solve anything. It will only make it worse." Caro stood her ground. She had to make Dell see before things got out of hand.

"I'm not going to beat him up, Caro, I'm going to kill him." Dell turned and she grabbed at his sleeve but missed.

"Dell!" Oh lord. Why did she tell him about what happened in her motor coach? Now he was going to go off and get into the kind of trouble that couldn't be solved with a fine or by taking away a trophy. Caro sighed and took out after him again.

She caught up to him seconds later around the corner of the garage. He'd come to a halt, and she saw he was talking to someone. She closed the distance between them.

"Out of my way, Dickey," Dell said as he tried to sidestep his half-brother.

"Wait, Dell." Warner put a hand on Dell's chest to stop him. Caro wanted to kiss him for slowing Dell down enough for her to catch up.

"I won't say it again," Dell warned.

"Look, Dell, news travels fast around here. I know what's going on, and I think you should hear me out. I may be able to help."

"Dell," Caro said. "Let's hear what Warner has to say. We could use all the help we can get right now." It was a testament to her desperation that she was willing to listen to anything one of Renfro's drivers had to say, especially this one. She didn't trust Warner as far as she could throw him.

"Unless he's here to tell us Renfro is dead, I don't want to hear it."

"Wait, Dell. Please. I think I can help," Warner said.

"Dell…" Caro pleaded.

"Spit it out. I haven't got all night."

"Is it true? About the fuel additive?"

"You came to find out if the rumors are true?" Dell shoved past Warner. "I don't fuckin' believe this." Caro lunged after him.

"Stop! Just stop for a damn minute. Let's hear him out."

It was a miracle. Dell stopped and turned around. "This better be good," he said.

"It's true? Someone put something in your gas can?"

Dell's whole body grew still. "Yeah," he drew the word out. "That seems like the most likely scenario."

"I think I know who might have done it."

"Who?" Caro tensed as the word spewed from Dell's lips like venom.

"You have a guy on your pit crew named Trent, right?"

"Yes," Caro answered. "He's one of the tire carriers."

"That's what I thought. He's new?"

Caro nodded. "We had to replace one of our carriers. He twisted an ankle playing softball."

"If he's the guy I'm thinking, he's a relative of Renfro's. A second cousin or nephew or something. I've seen him around our garage a time or two. He looks like a normal kid, but…" Warner ran a hand through his hair in a gesture that reminded Caro of Dell. "There's something about him. He smiles too much, if you know what I mean. It kind of creeps me out."

"I asked him to put a bottle of champagne in my locker for me," Dell said. He looked directly at Caro and said, "I was planning a private celebration, just you and me."

Caro smiled. She'd saved a bottle too, and for the same reason. "Is it still there?"

"I don't know. The hauler wasn't going anywhere for hours, so I wasn't in any rush to get it. I was going to find you first."

Caro tore her eyes away from Dell to the man watching them with undisguised humor. She no longer cared who knew Dell and she were together. Warner smiled and raised one hand.

"Hey, I'm happy for you. I wish I'd had the nerve to make a move on you before my brother did."

"No offense, but it wouldn't have made any difference." Caro wrapped her arm around Dell's waist and he did the same, snuggling her close. His body was still tense, but the rage was gone – for now. "Come on, let's go talk to the officials. I don't think they're going to reverse their decision, but we can try."

❧

"Stay here," Dell said. "I don't want you anywhere near Renfro ever again."

"You aren't going to keep me from seeing his face when he realizes he's been found out," Caro argued.

In the end, Dell couldn't stop her. The two of them followed a pack of AARA officials across the infield to Butch Renfro's motor coach. It was late, but the lights were on inside. No doubt, Butch was celebrating what he thought was the end of Hawkins Racing.

"Promise me you won't do anything stupid," Caro said as they approached.

"Define stupid," Dell said.

Caro's fingers on his forearm stopped him. "Please, Dell. This isn't funny. Don't give the officials a reason to sack you, or Renfro a reason to have you arrested." Dell wrapped her in his arms and held tight. She apparently knew him well, because that was exactly what he had in mind. But her pleading tone and the shimmer of tears in her eyes was enough to cut through the rage that had been building ever since he walked into the garage tonight and saw what was going on.

"I promise, Caro." His hands stroked her back as he pressed a kiss to the top of her head where it rested against his chest. "You're the only person who's ever cared enough to worry about me. It's sweet."

"I'm not being sweet, Dell, I'm being practical. I don't have money to bail my driver out of jail."

"Come on." He set her away with a kiss to her forehead. "Let's go. We don't want to miss all the fun."

Dell didn't expect Renfro to be happy to see him when he and Caro entered behind the officials, but he wasn't prepared for the thundercloud of hate that rolled off the man directly toward them. Dell put a protective arm around Caro and stared the man down.

"What are they doing here?" Renfro asked.

"We thought they had a right to be here," Stan said. Dell thought he might grow to like this Stan fellow, given time.

Renfro scowled. "What's this about?"

"We just had a talk with your nephew, Trenton Biggs. He told us everything."

"Well, I don't know what he said, but I wouldn't believe him. The kid's bad news. Why do you think he doesn't work for me?"

"But he does work for you," Stan said. "He's been working for you all season, and in exchange for his sabotaging Hawkins Racing, you paid off his mother's mortgage and back taxes."

Renfro dropped all pretense, rounding on Dell with a rage that had Dell shuffling Caro behind him. His face turned puce as he pointed a finger at Dell. "You. It's all your fault. You ruined my life, you miserable son-of-a-bitch."

"Whoa," Dell said, taken aback by Renfro's hatred. "What did I ever do to you?"

"You exist. That's enough. If it wasn't for you, she'd be mine."

"Oh no," Dell said. "Carolina would never be yours, and if you ever touch her again, I'll kill you."

"Dell," Caro hissed behind him.

"Shh, Caro," he said. "I won't let him hurt you again."

"I'm not talking about your bitch, Junior. I'm talking about your mother. I asked her to marry me, but she didn't want me. Caudell knocked her up and she married the bastard. I told her not to. Told her he couldn't keep his goddamned pecker in his pants, but did she listen to me? Hell no. She went ahead and married him, and the next thing you know, Pauline Warner shows up at the track with Caudell's bastard. Says she wants her man back. That's all it took. The next thing I know, Pauline and her whelp are hanging around, and Maggie was gone."

Dell absorbed the tirade. As horrible as it was, it had the ring of truth.

"So, you set out to destroy Hawkins Racing because of me?" Dell asked.

"Damn right I did. I hired Caudell's bastard and by damned if he didn't kill his old man for me. You should have seen his face when I told him Caudell was his sperm donor." Renfro's laugh made Dell's skin crawl. Caro clamped the back of his shirt in her fists and he wished to hell he hadn't let her come tonight as Renfro continued.

"Then the bastard went after you. I couldn't have scripted it better if I'd tried. I was trying to get that idiot, Trent, into Anderson's garage when Virgil wised up and fired your sorry ass. But you made it easy on me. You went over to the bitch's garage. I knew I had you then."

He was insane. Dell couldn't care less about the fact Butch Renfro wanted him dead, but he did care about Carolina. "Watch who you're calling names, Renfro. I'm not going to warn you again. Carolina hasn't done anything to earn your scorn."

"Dell," Caro warned.

"Let's go, Caro. I've heard enough." Dell ushered Caro out the door to Renfro's enraged shouts of, "It's all your fault".

Chapter Eighteen

"Just hear her out, okay?" Dell faced the solemn group gathered around the conference table at AARA's headquarters in Daytona Beach. The last forty-eight hours were sheer hell for Hawkins Racing, and AARA in general. Having one team sabotage another didn't do anything for the credibility of the sport, coupled with Renfro admitting to sexually assaulting Caro, and AARA was fighting a massive PR battle.

However, Dell hadn't felt this good – ever.

Renfro was certifiably crazy, and under arrest for a variety of charges, including assault on a AARA official after Dell left with Caro. As crazy as Renfro was, he'd answered a lot of questions for Dell and Dickey, and all Dell felt was relief. Later that night, with Caro wrapped in his arms, he'd found what he was looking for.

"Are you okay?" she asked.

"Yeah, I am. I always thought there couldn't be anything worse than having Caudell Wayne for a father, but I was wrong," he told her.

"How so?"

"Just think, if things had been different, Butch Renfro could have been my father."

"Thank God for small favors," Caro said.

"No, thank God for you."

So now he had a new cause, Caro Hawkins.

The officials gathered around the conference table represented the highest levels of ownership and management within the organization. Dell faced them as if they didn't have the power to end his career with the stroke of a pen.

"We aren't asking you to reverse your decision. We'll live with it. You did what you had to. But you need to see the data Ms. Hawkins compiled before and after the altered gas was put in the car. She's one hell of an automotive engineer, and she's built the best damned engine I've ever run. You owe it to yourself, and the sport to hear her out."

Caro sat quietly while Dell went around the table handing out the packets they'd hastily put together only this morning. Dell called in favors, mostly owed to his father, to get this meeting. She'd argued that he didn't need to do it, but Dell countered her objection, saying for once, he didn't mind trading on his old man's name. He figured Caudell owed him a favor or two.

"You can glance through the first few pages. You'll see the engine performance is steady, not much changes from one lap to another. I can tell you, she was running like a crazy – smooth as glass. So, go ahead, scan the graphs on those pages. Stop when you get to page eight." He looked down at Caro and smiled. "I think it would be better if Ms. Hawkins explains the graph on that page to you."

Caro stood, taking Dell's place. "As you can see, precisely four minutes before Dell's last pit stop, engine performance went up by seven percentage points. If you'll flip over to the next page, you'll see a detailed readout from the weather station at the track. At that exact time, a cold front came through. The track temperature dropped ten degrees in a matter of seconds. Now, if you'll turn back to the other page… do you see where the car pitted? "

Caro nodded at the murmurs around the room as they figured out the chart. "That's the stop where the altered gas was put into the car's fuel cell. Now, if you follow the timeline, you'll see Dell went back out on the track, and even though the track temperature was significantly lower than it was when he pitted, the car's performance, though elevated, was less than the seven percent improvement exhibited before the pit stop." She paused to let the men absorb what they were seeing.

"So, gentlemen, the data supports my conclusion that the additive actually produced a negative effect on the engine's performance, rather than a positive one. Dell won the race despite the additive, not because of it."

Caro sat. She gave Dell a brief smile. He reached over and took her hand in his and squeezed. Whatever they decided, Caro was okay with. As long as Dell believed in her, it didn't matter if no one else in the whole world did, and she was darned tired of letting other people dictate her private life.

&

Goddamn she was cute, Dell thought as he shook the bottle and sprayed champagne on Caro's scrunched up face. She'd told him more than once how much she hated this part of the Victory Lane celebration, but after their first win following the Talladega disaster, when he'd bathed her in champagne in Victory Lane, then minutes later took her to the hauler and proceeded to lick it off her skin, she'd come to tolerate it. For his sake, she said. She might not admit it, but behind those scrunched up eyelids, she was imagining his lips on her skin, making her squeal and moan as he drank champagne from her navel, celebrating, Dell Wayne style.

"Stop! Dell!," she protested with a laugh. "Enough!"

He passed the near-empty bottle to the closest person and tugged Caro close. She lowered her hands from her face and allowed him to brush the champagne from her eyelids with his thumbs. He followed that by kissing the champagne from her lips. She wrapped her arms around his neck and kissed him back as a chorus of whoops rose from the crowd.

When she pushed against his chest, he let her go, but not before brushing his lips across the shell of her ear and whispering, "I love you."

A reporter shoved a microphone in between them, and Dell shifted to face the reporter, holding Caro close, with an arm around her waist.

"Dell, your season got off to a rocky start, and here you are now, celebrating another win, and you're on your way to the Chase for the Championship. How do you feel about that?"

Dell gave Caro's hip a reassuring squeeze. They'd come a long way since Talladega, and he'd won more races, and had more decent finishes in the last half of the season than ever before in his career, but none of it mattered to him.

"For me to end up where I am right now is proof positive that anything is possible in AARA," Dell said. "I've got my work cut out for me in the next ten races. I can't let my brother win – that just wouldn't be right." Dell smiled and waved at Dickey who was waiting for his turn to congratulate the winner.

"Speaking of your brother, it's been quite a season for the two of you. Do you and Richard Warner have any plans to team up in the future?"

"I don't think so, but you'd have to ask him. He's a big-shot team owner now, and I'm just a lowly driver."

"Are the rumors true you loaned Richard the money to buy out Butch Renfro after AARA banned him from racing for tampering with your car?"

"I didn't *loan* Dickey anything," Dell said. He'd only given him what was rightfully his, half the remaining money he'd inherited from Caudell Senior. Given Renfro's desperate circumstances, the money was more than enough to buy him out and keep the garage running. But that was no one's business but theirs.

"So you have no plans to drive for Warner Racing next season?"

Oh, hell no! Dell frowned at the camera. "No, I don't. I drive for Carolina Hawkins, and no one else." He tugged her around, shifting at the same time so they stood face-to-face. He winked.

"Dell," she whispered, "what are you doing?"

"Cameron," he addressed the reporter, "if you'll forgive me, I have something I'd like to say." Dell didn't wait for the reporter's agreement, barreling on as if he had every right to hijack a national television broadcast. "I know this is highly improper, but I've fallen in love with my team owner." He turned his gaze to Carolina who stood, open-mouthed and wide-eyed. Damn, he hated to blind-side her this way, but he didn't want to wait another minute to tell the world how he felt about her, and claim her as his own. He smiled at her, then dropped to one knee on the champagne-soaked ground.

The crowd grew quiet, or maybe she couldn't hear them over the roar of blood rushing past her ears. Dell had a flair for the dramatic, but she never guessed he'd do something so foolish, and so sweet. He reached for her hands, and she held them out to him. He took them in his and placed a silly, smacking kiss on the back of each one. She laughed, despite the serious look Dell maintained. He looked up at her and she felt dizzy for the first time in her life. He squeezed her hands, and she steadied.

"Carolina, my sweet, Carolina, I love you, and not just because you build a wicked good engine. I love you, because from the beginning, you saw the real me, on and off the racetrack, and not someone you wanted me to be. You believed in me, even when I didn't believe in myself. You make me want to be a better man, Carolina. I promise to try every day to be the man you see inside this shell. Will you marry me?"

All seriousness gone, Dell's eyes twinkled with amusement and his wicked smile promised all sorts of things she'd come to need as much as she needed to breathe. Lord, if she said yes, this man would keep her off balance for the rest of her life. And wasn't that one of the things she loved most about him?

She forgot all about the reporters, the cameras and the crowd. Only one man mattered, and he'd chosen this moment to declare himself. Maybe, just maybe, she could keep him a little off balance too.

"I don't know, Dell. Are you sure you aren't just trying to get your hands on my engine?" she teased.

"Oh, honey, I fully intend to get my hands on every inch of you, including your engine," he said with a wink.

"Well...since you put it that way... yes!"

Dell let out a victory whoop and pulled her in for a kiss that curled her toes. The crowd went crazy around them, and someone dumped what felt like a magnum of champagne over their heads. Eventually, Dell broke the kiss, but he didn't let her go as he grabbed the microphone from the stunned reporter who was scrambling to keep up with the unexpected marriage proposal in Victory Lane.

"So, folks. Looks like I'm going to marry my team owner. Maybe I'll change my name to Caudell Hawkins, what do you think?"

The crowd roared their approval. Dell looked around, then waved someone over. Caro smiled as Richard Warner shouldered his way through the crowd. "Did you get it?" Dell asked his brother.

"Yeah," he said, handing something to Dell. "You've got to quit ordering people around," he added with a smile. He clapped Dell on the back. "Congratulations, man." Then he faded back into the crowd.

"Sorry, sweetheart. I couldn't figure out a way to carry this in the car with me and not lose it." Caro's heart lodged in her throat when Dell opened the small velvet box to reveal the most stunning diamond she'd ever seen. "You can have this, or if you'd prefer, I'll give you the guitar trophy I just won," he said. "But, so you know, I come with both of them. You aren't getting away from me now."

And there she was, completely off balance, and dizzy with love for this impossible man.

"Sweet Carolina," he waved the ring under her nose. "Which will it be?"

Caro eyed the unique trophy awarded at Richmond. She studied the ring in its blue velvet box. "As much as I love the trophy, Dell, you can keep it. I'll take the ring, and you."

Dell slid the ring on her finger, then crushed her lips beneath his. As he kissed her senseless, she heard the reporter say, "And there you have it folks. This wraps up our coverage today from Richmond International Raceway in beautiful, Richmond, Virginia, where Dell Wayne is a double winner today – taking home the winner's trophy and a bride!"

ABOUT THE AUTHOR

USA Today Best-Selling author Roz Lee is the author of twenty-five romances. The first, The Lust Boat, was born of an idea acquired while on a Caribbean cruise with her family and soon blossomed into a five book series published by Red Sage. Following her love of baseball, she turned her attention to sexy athletes in tight pants, writing the critically acclaimed Mustangs Baseball series.

Roz has been married to her best friend, and high school sweetheart, for nearly four decades. Roz and her husband have two grown daughters, a son-in-law, and are the proud grandparents to the cutest little boy ever.

Even though Roz has lived on both coasts, her heart lies in between, in Texas. A Texan by birth, she can trace her family back to the Republic of Texas. With roots that deep, she says, "You can't ever really leave."

When Roz isn't writing, she's reading, or traipsing around the country on one adventure or another. No trip is too small, no tourist trap too cheesy, and no road unworthy of travel.

Roz is a member of New Jersey Romance Writers, Los Angeles Romance Authors, Liberty State Fiction Writers, Sisters in Crime, and the Authors Guild.

www.RozLee.net
Twitter - @RozLee_Author
Facebook - Authorrozlee

OTHER TITLES BY ROZ LEE

Lone Star Honky Tonk Series
Lookin' Good
Hung Up
Rockin' O
Barbed Wire

Mustangs Baseball Series
Inside Heat
Going Deep
Bases Loaded
Switch Hitter
Spring Training
Strike Out
Free Agent
Seasoned Veteran

Lesbian Office Romance Series
A Spanking Good Christmas
Special Delivery Valentine
Pushing the Envelope
Yours, Thankfully

Billionaire Brides Series
The Backdoor Billionaire's Bride
The Yankee Billionaire's Bride
The Reluctant Billionaire Bride

Lothario Series
The Lust Boat
Show Me the Ropes
Love Me Twice
Four of Hearts
Under the Covers

Also:
Suspended Game
Still Taking Chances
Banged on Broadway
The Middlethorpe Chronicles
Hearts on Fire
Summer Sizzle Anthology

Roz Lee